C000037519

AISHA

&

JOHN

A NOVEL

by

OLU BALOGUN.

1ST Edition.

LAGOS

Theories of Freedom publications, Lekki.

2019.

Dedication

To Her, who
helped me
experience deep
emotions and gave
me her Self to
obsess about – 'Z'

To Him, who
always forgave me
whenever I wrote
him a letter,
because he loved
my writing – 'S'

CHAPTER 1

It's a Friday afternoon, just some minutes after twelve noon, as Aisha Mustapha's driver parks outside the Lekki Central Mosque. The crowd of people gradually make their way into the large compound of the Mosque, passing by various merchants. It's time for the customary Jumu'ah; the congregational Friday prayer.

Aisha steps out of the black Mercedes S class, dressed in a white Abaya, escorted by her two security guards. Her father married eight wives, with her mother being the fifth wife. Aisha is the last child of her mother's five children and the only daughter of her mother.

She bows her head down and walks in a manner reflecting religious piety. She's always been a beacon of Islamic virtue to the people around her, since she was a little girl, mostly because her father was a well-respected member of the Muslim community of Nigeria, and now all over the World. Her mother, who was born in Saudi Arabia, shares family ties with the King of Saudi Arabia, being his distant niece.

She swings her purple Dolce & Gabbana Hijab over her shoulders, putting it securely in place. Her father, Alhaji (Dr.) Aliu Mustapha, has never let his children be without luxury. He is a pious man himself and has never shown to put his faith in material things but he was born into an immensely wealthy family and has gone even further to expand his inheritance with various international investments. He graduated from the Harvard Business School in nineteen seventy-six, after which he was given a large amount of capital and assets, by his father, to invest with. He did an excellent job and within a year he had almost doubled what he was given.

Aisha walks into the compound gate, with her two personal guards; Nuru and Abu. They both started working for her, under her dad, about a year ago, just some weeks after all the members of her family underwent the life-changing event. She makes eye contact with a few familiar faces within the compound and smiles cordially in return, as she enters. Most of her family had to relocate to Kano a year ago but she was insistent on staying in Lagos. She ended up staying back along with her older brother Usman, who is married with one beautiful child.

Ever since Aisha got back from her two-year stay in the UK, a year ago, she has worked in her father's mobile telecommunications company, alongside Usman. She just left the office at Victoria Island, forty minutes ago, so she could make it in time for prayer.

The Muezzin; the person appointed to recite the call to prayer, sings out the mandatory call for Muslims, to worship. As it is written in the Qur'an; 'O ye who believe! When the call is proclaimed to prayer on Friday, hasten earnestly to the remembrance of Allah, and leave off business'. When she was younger, her mother would sometimes read her teachings from various Hadith; reports about the words, actions and habits of the Prophet, Muhammad. Lots of those teachings remain with her and amongst them, one of the most visual is of the Angels said to be standing at the gates of the mosque, recording the names of people as they entered, in order of the time they entered. It always made her understand how important the Jumu'ah is to Allah.

She collects her prayer mat from Nuru, one of her two guards, before leaving them to join the women in their allotted space.

The Muezzin has started singing the second call, for Muslims to line up for the beginning of prayers. She takes off her shoes and then unrolls her mat before laying it on the clean floor. Aisha had already performed her ablution just before leaving her office. Her whole body is well covered; only her palms and face are visible. Back when her father was still residing in Lagos, she would sometimes sit with him at the front of the congregation, along with her mother, because of his position in the Muslim community and his selfless giving, but after the sudden change of events last year, her father and most of her family has relocated to, and remained in Kano. Ordinarily, it is mostly forbidden for the male and female to sit or pray beside each other in the mosques, except they are related by blood.

Aisha is already facing the right direction; at the center of the mosque in Mecca is the Ka'ba, towards which all Muslims around the world are to face when praying. The prayers are about to start.

She stands straight on her mat and makes her intentions known to Allah, within her heart. She then raises her hands to her ears and says in Arabic; "Allah is the greatest."

She places her left palm over her breasts, places the right palm on top of it and recites the opening prayer. As is customary, she does not let her eyes stray but sometimes, the mind does wander about. Her thoughts are with her father as she recites the prayers; she is thankful to Allah for the sacred opportunity given to her father a year ago, to become the new Emir of Kano. She is thankful for having such an inspiring figure to look up to; such a selfless giver, who always grants her what she needs and more.

She places her palms on her knees and bends her back to a ninety-degree angle, while keeping her legs straight and says in Arabic; "glorious is my Lord, the most great", three times and then stands back up. Her mind wanders to her fiancé now; Hassan. He is the third son of her father's longtime friend; General Ibrahim. Hassan was the only son who joined the Nigerian military, like his father, and has now risen to the rank of Major, at the age of thirty. Aisha is twenty-seven years old and has been betrothed to Hassan since she was sixteen. They have both become friends over the years and she almost has no reason to refuse his hand in marriage. He is just three years older than her, he is handsome, knowledgeable and well-travelled, but he does have his dark side. She knows he keeps other girls on the side, even though he has never disrespected her by bringing any of them around her. She is aware that Hassan might end up with more than one wife, just like her father did, but she knows very well that Hassan does not have the wisdom or patience to handle polygamy, like her father.

She asks Allah to give her a stable and loving family of her own.

She crouches down and places her forehead, palms and knees on the floor together, while saying; "Allāhu akbar." She plans to spend the coming Sunday afternoon with Hassan at the Polo Club in Ikoyi and maybe, onto the evening, if he has something planned. He can be spontaneous and fun sometimes but at other times, he could take it too far and become suicidal.

Two weeks ago, he suddenly came up with the crazy idea to go to South Africa for the weekend and return by Sunday evening, so she decided to go with the flow. It was a lot of fun sight-seeing and then going clubbing; dancing freely, like she could never do in Nigeria. No one recognized her as the daughter of Alhaji Mustapha or the daughter of the new Emir of Kano. She still put on her Hijab at the club but she wore a beautiful body-hugging dress and some of the expensive jewelry her mother gave her. It was all fun until some guy approached her and asked her to dance. She respectfully declined the offer but the young man was very drunk and a little too persistent. Hassan then lost it; he grabbed the guy by the neck and pinned him to the table. He then poured all the contents of a champagne bottle into his mouth and all over his face. The young man was overpowered by Hassan, who had undergone years of rigorous military training but that didn't stop five of his friends from rushing to his rescue. A chaotic fight ensued at the club; Hassan picked up more bottles and smashed them on the heads of two of the friends before the club security could intervene. Right in his eyes, Aisha could see the bloodlust; he was enjoying the violence.

Hassan knew the club manager quite well, so the young man and his five friends were thrown out. Luckily for them, no passer-by took pictures and the scandal was concealed.

The prayers gradually come to an end. She is seated on the floor, with her right knee bent backwards and her left foot crossed under her right leg. She says her personal prayers to Allah; "give me wisdom to face the coming week and show me the truth. Bless my family and keep us all from harm."

To end her prayer, she turns to her head to the right and says in Arabic; "the Angel who records your good deeds is to this side". She then turns her head to left and says in Arabic; "the Angel who records your bad deeds is on this side."

*****

The church bus pulls up in front of the main entrance and Father John gets into the front passenger seat, wearing his white Cassock. The two deacons behind him get in at the back of the bus.

"Where to Father?" asks the bus driver; Nnamdi.

"We need to pick up some supplies for the Bazaar tomorrow; let's go to the Buy-Right Supermarket at Victoria Island."

"Okay, Father."

"Or what do you think, Benedict?" John asks, looking back at one of the deacons.

"I agree with you, Father. Buy-Right is a large Supermarket and would probably have everything on our list."

"Okay. Wonderful," John says contentedly.

Nnamdi drives the Bus out of the gate of the Church of Assumption, Ikoyi, and onto the Falomo roundabout. He then climbs onto the bridge leading to Victoria Island. It's one-thirty in the afternoon and the sun is high up. It is another hot afternoon in the city of Lagos but the air-conditioning in the new church bus is more than enough to keep them cool.

Father John is only twenty-seven years old but he has already joined the priesthood, after four years in the seminary and a two more as a deacon. He graduated from the University of Lagos, just over seven years ago, where he studied Philosophy, and went straight into the seminary, after his youth service. A vacuum in his heart drove him towards this path and he has filled it with a new purpose.

Just last month, he underwent his Rite of Ordination. During the Holy Mass, he was called forward by the Bishop and was presented to the congregation.

After a few interrogatory questions, he was asked to lie prostrate while the whole church prayed for him. Thereafter the Bishop laid hands on him and invoked the power of the Holy Spirit. He was then given the sacred priestly garments; the Stole and Chasuble.

Fortunately for them, they left just at the right time; that time when the Victoria Island traffic is just building but has not yet gained momentum. There are many cars on the road, heading in the same direction but they have not been pulled into a halt yet. The traffic light ahead stays green and it seems it just turns yellow just after the church bus passes the Oriental Hotel intersection. They drive off the main road and turn into the street leading to the Buy-Right Supermarket.

Ever since John entered the Priesthood it seems he has been walking on a divine cloud. One could call it 'good luck following him' but he will describe it as the power of the Holy Spirit directing his every step to perfection. Everyone in his life has also raised the level of respect they give to him; they now address him as 'Father', they avoid too much eye contact with him and listen rapturously whenever he opens his mouth to talk. In his most private thoughts he remembers those people who never wanted him to attain this level of authority. He has now become a Diocesan Priest.

He will never forget how the presiding Archbishop of his Archdiocese; the Most Reverend Tayo Adekunle, took one look at him and saw his potential; he saw the earnestness of his spirit; he saw John's dedication to love. If there was any self-doubt in John, Bishop Tayo Adekunle helped to root it out, with his righteous guidance.

Nnamdi parks the Bus inside the large compound of the Buy-Right Supermarket. Father John, Deacon Benedict and Deacon Babatunde step out of the bus. They walk in an orderly manner into the building, calling the attention of Faithfuls all around.

A young lady, holding her packaged groceries, calls out to them; "Father John! Good afternoon!"

"Good afternoon! God bless you!" John replies, with a bright smile. They enter the building and head straight into the Supermarket.

Deacon Benedict unrolls the piece of paper in his hand containing the 'Shopping List'.

"Grab a basket each and let's get this over with quickly," he says to both deacons, "the traffic would soon start building and we mustn't be late to return."

They both pull out rolling trolleys and push them behind him. He heads towards the Stationary section first, to pick up the set of exercise books and pens needed by the volunteers, to record the sales as they happen tomorrow.

The Bazaar is being organised and managed by him. You can call it his first major responsibility since becoming a Priest. As with everything he lays his hands to do, it must be a success. This is a great way to raise money for the church, which would be used in the continual furtherance of the Ministry. He also knows that demonstrating the skill to call money out when needed is something to be revered amongst all members of the Priesthood. It speaks of a resemblance to the Lord Jesus Christ, who always found the way to summon what was needed.

"John?" comes the voice that almost seems to shatter his well-constructed thoughts. Her voice sounds so familiar, though he dares not place a face to it until he turns to look at her. He gracefully turns towards the lady addressing him by his first name, with no title attached. His deacons also look towards the lady, scoldingly.

"Aisha..." replies John, with his mind trailing off into a well-preserved collection of thoughts. She approaches him cautiously, while her two guards Nuru and Abu stand in the same spot, stone-faced. She can't help but notice his clothing as she gathers in his presence.

"It's been... more than seven years since I saw you..." she says softly.

"Yes, it has," he says, regaining his Priestly demeanor, "what a nice surprise. How are you doing?"

She snaps out of her ghostly stare too. "I'm doing great! Are you now a Pastor?"

"A Priest; I guess you can call it 'Pastor'. I heard the great news; your Dad."

"Yes," she says confidently, "he was the next in-line after his Grandfather died, so he's now the Sultan of Kano."

"He truly deserves it. He has always been a devoted man... and your brothers? Kabiru, Usman and –"

"They're fine. Kabiru is in Kano now but Usman is still in Lagos - we work together at Vodasat Telecoms – and my two other brothers are in Abuja..." She finds herself not saying what she truly feels like saying.

He delves into those thoughts again as he stares into those beautiful eyes of hers. She was always so eye-catching, covered from head to toe, in her Hijab and Abaya. Her face and palms were enough to convince you of her resplendent beauty.

She suddenly smiles as they keep eye contact. "So, what are you doing here?"

He hesitates to answer, as though he can't remember.

Deacon Benedict cuts in; "we are here to get supplies for our Bazaar tomorrow at the Church of Assumption. Myself, Deacon Babatunde and *Father* John are overseeing the organization of the event."

Aisha stretches her palm towards Benedict. "Hello, I'm Aisha, nice to meet you." He collects her hand courteously.

"Thank you, Deacon Benedict," John finally says. He turns to her. "It was great running into you."

Aisha takes that as the end of their coincidental meeting. "Yes, it was."

"You should come to our Bazaar tomorrow. Lots of nice items to pick up!" Benedict says, switching to his marketer-mode.

"I am sure she has plans for tomorrow." John turns to Aisha. "Never mind, you don't -"

"Am I not invited?" she asks John, almost insulted.

"...of course, you are... we would love to have you," he utters.

"Okay then. I'll be there." She then turns to Benedict and asks; "what time?"

"It starts at two p.m.," Benedict replies.

"Great. I'll clear out my schedule for tomorrow..." she concludes, looking into John's eyes. He looks back, trying to understand what she's thinking. "Let me leave you to get back to your shopping. See you tomorrow... Father John and Deacon Benedict." She gives a courteous smile to Deacon Babatunde.

John smiles in response and bows his head a little as she turns to leave. He then turns to Benedict, in an almost-scolding manner and asks; "what do we have on the list?"

CHAPTER 2

It was in the month of August, two thousand and eleven, that Aisha Mustapha celebrated her nineteenth birthday. Her whole nuclear family happened to be in Lagos; even her senior brother, Usman, who was back on vacation from school in the UK. Her two oldest brothers, Bashir and Danladi, also came into town from Abuja, leaving their official duties at the Ministry of Transportation and the Ministry of Health, respectively. However, everyone didn't converge because of Aisha's birthday, they did so because their dad was taking a holiday trip to Saudi Arabia, along with his fifth wife; Karida; their mother. It was a long overdue holiday for their dad and her children were happy to see him go, especially with their mother, who had been complaining to them of feeling neglected by him. Karida had summoned her two eldest sons from Abuja; Bashir and Danladi, to let them know about the changes that were likely to come and what they must do to ensure everyone in their family remained protected.

Alhaji (Dr.) Aliu Mustapha had always been the prime choice to replace his Grandfather, the Emir of Kano, among all the members in his family tree. He had been an upstanding Muslim all his life and had gathered a great amount of respect from Muslims all over Nigeria, and beyond, for his charitable deeds. In addition, he had, by coincidence or by choice, married a member of the Saudi Arabian royal family; his fifth wife Karida, who was the last daughter of the new King's half-sister.

Just last week, Alhaji Aliu Mustapha's grandfather, the Emir of Kano, was flown out to Dubai for emergency healthcare. The Emir was a man in his early nineties and he had seen his fair share of life. It looked like he would be dying soon and a lot of people had shifted their minds to Alhaji Aliu Mustapha, as the next in line for the throne. However, it wasn't going to be that easy. The Emir had about eighteen children, among whom were five sons. Two of his sons had died; Alhaji Aliu Mustapha's father; Musa and the Emir's eldest son, leaving three uncles and their respective sons, for Aliu to contend with.

Karida had planned the impromptu trip to Saudi Arabia with her husband, under the guise of a 'holiday', so they could spend a week at the Murabba Palace, in Riyadh, where King Al-Aziz was staying presently. Her plan was to setup a meeting between her husband and the King, and give him a chance to convince the King that he was the meritorious choice for the position of Sultan of Kano, believing that the support of the Saudi Arabian King would seal her husband's ascension to the throne. In the meantime, she had to keep all members of her household out of the view of antagonists and away from harm's way. It was common knowledge that Aliu's uncles were very violent men, who wouldn't mind taking their late brother's son's life or his children's lives, if it meant taking the throne for themselves. It was quite evident with the number of death threats that had been spewed out of their mouths. It was a period of high-tension, which could only be assuaged when the final decision for the next Emir had been indisputably made.

According to the will of the ailing Emir, his grandson, Aliu, was to be his successor but in matters like these, that rest so heavily on the destinies of many men, a dying man's will was not always enough to put the opposing powers to rest.

It was nighttime, just some hours before Aisha's birthday, when Karida called for Bashir and Danladi. They went to meet with her and their father privately, in the master bedroom. All five children were in the main parlor at the time, still reveling in the feeling of being together, under one roof, after such a long time; they had all missed each other.

Bashir and Danladi ascended the staircase, responding to their mother's call, while the other three continued catching up; Usman, Kabiru and Aisha. The baby of the house; Aisha, was at the same time exchanging heart-soothing text messages with her secret lover; John, telling him all about the family reunion and making plans for her private birthday party, taking place somewhere on their university campus, tomorrow evening.

*****

"Allāhu akbar!" sings the Muezzin, at the Mustapha's Lagos residence's private Mosque. Aisha wakes up to the sound. It is just five, forty-six in the morning; time for today's Fajr prayer.

She steps out of bed, happy that today is a Saturday. She only has to swing by the office in Victoria Island for an hour or two, to finish up a presentation, and then she has the rest of the day to herself.

She goes over to ease herself in the bathroom and then brushes her teeth. One of the first thoughts on her mind, after waking up, is the bazaar today at John's church. It is dawning on her that it's going to be a little odd, being at a Catholic church, in her regular Muslim attire, but she didn't consider that when insisting on going. For some moments, during the encounter with him at the Supermarket, she traveled back in time, to seven-almost-eight years ago, when she and John were indisputably on the same side. Wherever you spotted her Hijab around the University, you would probably see a tall and gentle-looking boy standing besides, by the name of John. They became best friends and in due course, lovers.

She gets ready to perform her ablution, before prayer. She turns on the tap to fill a white bowl with water.

Now, she can't really tell if she and John are on the same side and she's not sure if they should be on the same side, but she can't forget that she owes him, and herself; an unfeigned apology for abandoning all the dreams they had created together.

"Bismillah," she says, after shutting the tap. She steps into her bathroom, still dressed, with the bowl of water beneath her. She then rinses her palms, from the fingertips to the wrist, three times. Maybe that's why she insisted on going to the Bazaar; it felt like coincidence granting her a chance to right her wrongs. She knows John felt wronged, even though she almost didn't have a choice in the matter but by consequence of all the promises they had made to each other, she undeniably broke her word.

She rinses her mouth three times. She rinses her nostrils three times. She uses her two palms to wash her face three times.

She continues, washing her hands from the fingers to the elbows, three times, starting with the right hand and then on to the left. The Bazaar is at two p.m.; she wonders if it's better to go a little early or very late. If early, she'll have to bear all the inquisitive Christian eyes, wondering how she missed her way, or even worse, someone recognizing the Emir's daughter and going to tattletale all about town. If late, she'll miss the chance to build a conversation with him, up to the point of apologizing, and so it would end up being a wasted effort.

She concludes her Ablution, sitting on the edge of her bath tub, by washing her legs, from the tiptoes to the ankle, three times, starting with the right leg and then on to the left. She finishes her cleansing and says in Arabic, ready for prayer; "I bear witness that none has the right to be worshiped but Allah alone, Who has no partner; and I bear witness that Muhammad is His slave and His messenger."

She dries herself with a small towel and steps into her bath slippers. She goes back into her room and pulls out her prayer mat. Sometimes she would go downstairs to pray with other inhabitants of the large compound, in their private Mosque; like some of her half brothers and sisters, workers and sometimes, her stepmothers. Today, she wants to be alone.

She lays her mat in the direction of the Qibla, takes off her slippers and steps on it, just as the Muezzin finishes the second call to prayer. She stands upright, opens her palms and raises them to her ears, before saying; "Allāhu akbar."

*****

The church bazaar has been officially started, for over an hour now. Many of the church members have already arrived, especially the youths. A few dedicated members of the Youths Church were given the sales stands to man. Church members donated a lot of items which they felt could be sold at the bazaar, in order to raise money for the church.

There are a lot of food and drink vendors present, along with a deejay, to ensure everyone gets filled and has fun. The Catholics are usually not very strict when it comes to entertainment. Mature members of the church feel comfortable enough to smoke a few cigarettes and have a couple of beers, or a cocktail, all within sensible limits. Friends and couples stand up to dance, while the Deejay is licensed to play the latest party hit-songs, and everyone ends up having a real blast.

Father John walks around the environs of the church compound, taking a distant look at the activities. He also can't deny that he has checked the group of people three times, to see if Aisha Mustapha had arrived. Other than that, he's also been thinking about the events of the morning.

It was seven days ago when they received the news of the death of Archbishop Dele Fatugba; the Metropolitan of the Ibadan Catholic Archdiocese. It usually doesn't take more than eight days to fill an Episcopal See; especially one as noticeable as the Archdiocese of Ibadan, and it didn't. News coming in this morning ended the period of *Sede Vacante* for seat of the Ibadan Archbishop but filled John's heart with disappointment.

The letter received this morning by Archbishop Tayo Adekunle, of the Lagos Archdiocese, confirmed that the College of Consultors had decided to transfer him to Ibadan, to oversee that Episcopal See.

The Most Reverend Tayo Adekunle was and will always be his spiritual father; it was through him that John was birthed into this new life of dedication. It would be sad to watch him leave but it is all in the service of the Lord. The Ecclesiastical Province of Ibadan has five other dioceses under it, while Lagos has just two, so in a way it is an increase in responsibility. To whom much is given, much is expected and Archbishop Adekunle has always been willing and ready to deliver.

What really troubled John was the promotion of Bishop Alexander Williams, to the seat of the Lagos Archdiocese, making him the Metropolitan of Lagos. John would have preferred any other member of Clergy to get that promotion but this was not in his control and for some reason the College of Consultors made that decision.

He had heard so many rumors about the Bishop, being involved in fraudulent financial dealings and in adulterous affairs with some esteemed married women in the church. A family of one such women ceased coming to the church, just some months ago.

Bishop Alexander had always been a showboat; utilizing his good looks and articulate speech to take more than he was supposed to get. In his heart, John had resisted judging the Bishop, as it is a sin to do so without hard knowledge of the fact, but after hearing his appointment to the height of this Episcopal See, he was forced to think like every other Faithful would; he was disappointed in the church politics.

He spots a black Mercedes S class pull into the church compound. The vehicle begins circling the compound, looking for a convenient parking space. John has been walking around the church compound, with his hands folded behind his back, and soon enough the Black Mercedes passes right beside him. It then stops, just after passing him by and reverses.

Aisha winds down the back window. "Hi!" she chimes, happy to have him be the first person she meets here.

"Hi... Aisha," John returns.

She steps down from the vehicle, wearing denim blue jeans, a long sleeve, white linen top, a blue, silk Hijab, and black sporty shoes, with black socks. Quite casual but a closer look and one will notice that she covered every part of her body, except for her face and palms.

"I'm quite glad to run into you", she says jovially, I was just thinking of how I was going to ask to see you and also how odd I would look with my Hijab among everyone.

He giggles. "You just ask to see 'Father John', not so hard, and you have no reason to feel odd; lots of our Sisters here dress similarly, with head covering. They're called Nuns."

She laughs. "Thanks... nice try at making me feel at home. At least you put in an effort, so others other might try the same."

"It's a really friendly environment - listen! ...they're even playing Tekno's latest song." She laughs again. He continues; "everyone is very accommodating here; you're free to have fun and fraternize."

"Okay. That's good... so we might have some time to talk later?"

He is hesitant; he would rather not open any old wounds. "...sure. Before you leave."

"Great... so, I'll just start the shopping now," she says, walking backwards, away from him, "I am sure you have a lot of responsibilities, and I'll ask for 'Father John' before I leave."

He smiles cordially, watching her back away. "How long are you here for?"

She looks at her watch; it's three-thirty in the afternoon. "Probably till six – definitely leaving before seven," she says, preparing to turn around. Her two guards, Nuru and Abu, step out of the car parked close by and walk towards her. Nuru drove them here.

"I'll probably find you before then," he confirms.

She smiles, clutching her handbag, ready to head towards the activities. "That will be nice."

He looks her straight in the eyes for the first time, briefly, as she turns around and walks away. Even a second of looking into those pools that are her eyes, bring back so many vivid feelings.

*****

Aisha woke long after the Fajr prayers had ended. She stayed up late last night, trading memories with her brothers and receiving birthday wishes via text and social media, from friends. The first person to wish her a happy birthday was John, even before her brothers who were present, because they had been chatting since eight p.m. and because he wanted to be the first to do so. She then slept at three a.m., after having a one-hour phone call with him, in the confines of her bedroom, just after her brothers had gone to bed.

She did hear the Muezzin's call to prayer around five a.m. but she knew she had the luxury of being lazy today because it was her birthday.

This was one of the best parts of her birthday; the early morning, when her mother would come into her room alone, pray for her and then give her a mind-blowing present. Her mother always found a way to make this year's gift much more memorable than last year's; it's been that way for all her previous eighteen birthdays and she couldn't wait to see what her mother would give for her nineteenth birthday. She heard a knock on the door; the sound of metal gold rings on thick wood, and she knew it was her mother.

She sat up in bed, excited. Karida entered, smiling brightly at her only daughter, holding a medium-sized gift bag.

"Happy birthday to you!" Karida sang.

CHAPTER 3

The five Invigilators walked around the large Exam hall, packed with over three hundred students, taking the African History, General Studies course. John had failed the course in his first year at the University of Lagos and now he decided to get it over and done with in his third year. He really shouldn't have failed it the first time but he was having a little too much fun in his 'freshite' days, and ended up arriving at the exam hall five minutes to the end; the invigilators didn't let him in. Now he is forced to take the course again, among the new freshites.

It was October of two thousand and nine, and John was at this same period writing his three hundred level, second semester exams. He had stayed up all night for two days, preparing for this annoying African History exam that cast a stumbling block in his way two years ago, making sure it would be a walk in the park.

He shaded away with his pencil, knowing the exact answer to each of the one hundred objective questions. The girl beside him seemed lost; she had not even finished her first ten questions and she kept erasing her choices and shading something new.

John looked over at her answer sheet and couldn't help but notice her pretty hands, which she used to handle her pencil and eraser smartly. She was wearing a wine-red Hijab and a black Abaya. She noticed his point of vision and looked at him. Their eyes met and he couldn't help but notice how pretty her face was. They both quickly looked away as one of the invigilators made a turn in their direction.

John was on his seventy-fourth question and he was dashing towards the finish line. The invigilator passed them by and walked further down the hall.

"Do you need my help?" John whispered to the girl beside him.

Aisha hesitated to answer. She looked around the hall to confirm there was no invigilator close by, first. "Yes, I do... but I don't want to get caught... better to fail." She swung her eyes towards him and smiled.

"Don't worry, I don't want to get caught either... let's exchange question papers."

"But they rearranged -"

"Don't worry, I'll circle the answers on your own question paper," he explained.

"Oh-okay." She took a look around; the coast was still clear. They then exchanged question papers. Aisha prayed in her heart to Allah that they wouldn't be caught. John took out twenty minutes to hurriedly circle the right choices of all her one hundred questions.

*****

Karida was seated on Aisha's bed, praying for her, asking for blessings from Allah as her daughter turned nineteen. She had stayed up late last night, telling her oldest sons, Bashir and Danladi, what must be done and how they must all conduct themselves from now on, to avoid the unwanted from the growing number of people who didn't wish them well. She didn't want to have to discuss that with her daughter but she had asked Bashir, the oldest son, to have a talk with his younger siblings.

"...ya Allah, please... please give Aisha more strength and patience to face all the challenges that lie ahead of her... please help Aisha in the days of the year ahead, that it may be her best year yet. Ya Allah, thank u... maybe all these 'thank you' would never be enough, but still... Ya Allah, thank u."

"Aamiin," Aisha concurred.

Her mother let go of her hand, smiling. "I got you something special for your nineteenth birthday." Karida pulled out a rectangular box wrapped in gift paper and handed it to her. Aisha collected the present, with her heart racing, and began to unwrap it.

"Can't wait to see it!" she exclaimed. She found a black suede box inside. She lifted the top open and was mesmerized by the beauty of the contents.

"You're now a woman, so I thought you should have your first set of expensive jewelry."

"I love it..." Aisha lifted the diamond clustered, platinum necklace, entranced. "Can I put it on?" she asked her mom, still in awe of the gift.

"Of course, it's yours." They both stood off the bed. Aisha walked over to her mirror, holding the jewelry box. Her mother collected the necklace and placed it over her head gently, before clasping it. "You should wear this when you go out to celebrate with Hassan. Let him see how beautiful his future wife is."

Aisha almost cringed at the thought of Hassan Ibrahim. She had been betrothed to him since she was sixteen but even now, three years later, she had not been able to open her heart to him. Now she was sure she wanted to marry John and no one else. It's him she wanted to show off her new jewelry to.

"Has he made plans with you yet?" her mother asked, as she collected the earrings also.

"Yes... he wanted to take me out for dinner at the Golden Gate tonight but I explained to him that I have three tests lined up for tomorrow, so we pushed it to Saturday."

"That's just two days away." Karida put the earrings on her and stared over her shoulder, at her reflection in the mirror.

"Yes..." Aisha thought about confiding in her mother about the issues of her troubled heart. "Mom, what... if I don't want to marry Hassan?"

Karida was taken aback. "Why not?"

"I... don't think I'm in love with him."

"Love takes time to grow, my dear. I know he is not as wise as your father yet but he will grow into a strong man. His father is an admirable man too and your father's old friend."

"But what if... I don't want him?"

"Then, my daughter, I will stand by your decision. I can't speak for your father but you can be sure I will be by your side... is that what you want?"

Aisha was happy that her mother understood but she took a second to consider her next words; "I'm not sure yet."

"Be sure before you make such a decision, okay?"

"Yes, mother."

"Good. I need to go and finish packing for the flight this afternoon," Karida said, heading out of the room, "I have asked Zainab to make you a lovely breakfast, then you can read for your tests at home, if you don't want to go to school today."

"I'll be going to school," she retorted, quite sharply.

"Okay." Karida left.

Aisha really did have a test the next day but the only reason why she wanted to go to school was because of the party John was throwing her at his uncle's house, which happened to be on campus, as his uncle was a senior lecturer.

His uncle, who was over fifty and still unmarried, had traveled for a Lecturer's Conference in the UK and John was the only one left at his staff quarters. He had brought up the fun idea of throwing her a private party, with just a few close friends, at the empty university staff house. Aisha loved the idea and was looking forward to one evening of unbridled freedom. She had invited three of her closest female friends in school; Ijeoma, Amina and Funke.

She heard another knock on the door. "Come in," she said.

Her four brothers filed in, smiling; first Kabiru, then Usman, Danladi and then the oldest, Bashir. "Happy birthday to you... happy birthday to you," they sang, each holding wrapped presents. Kabiru's eyes popped when he saw the diamond jewelry set on her.

"Wow!" he exclaimed, interrupting the singing and dashing forward to take a closer look. The other brothers also turned their attention. "Mummy won't give me this kind of present o," Kabiru whined. Aisha laughed.

"See my small sister looking like a Queen!" Usman chimed, proud. Aisha blushed, comically walking on an imaginary fashion runway.

"Beautiful!" Bashir exclaimed. "Hope you will manage our own presents" he said, handing her his. The other three brothers also handed her theirs. She managed to hold all four presents in her hands.

"Thank you all. I appreciate your gifts," she said, trying hard to console them, while sparkling in her diamonds.

"So, where's the party?!" Kabiru asked her.

"Which party? There's no party; I have tests tomorrow, abeg."

"Daddy and Mummy are travelling..." Kabiru said, giving a mischievous look to his brothers, "let's go clubbing tonight."

"That's precisely *not* what we're going to do," Danladi asserted, sternly.

"Let's all talk," Bashir said, going back to shut Aisha's door. The others knew their eldest brother, who was twenty-seven years old, had something important to say. Danladi was the only one who seemed aware of the upcoming topic. Bashir returned. "From now on, we have to be very careful where we go and the company we keep. Our Dad has informed me that he is most likely going to be the next Sultan of Kano -

"Wow!" Kabiru shouted, excited.

"Especially you, Kabiru." Bashir turns to him. "You have to really change. We all know you're the black sheep of this family; fighting, having accidents with the cars and reports of being seen drunk all over town! We can't afford that anymore. Right now, you need to look after your younger sister and keep her out of trouble." He then turned his face to the others. "We all need to act more appropriately, everywhere we go; we're about to become royalty and that is going to come with a lot of enemies. People will look for every weak spot and poke at it. Some people are even threatening our lives as we speak! There are other people, contending dad's claim to the throne, even though the Emir has named him. Right now, the Emir is very sick and if he dies, things will really get heated up! The doctors say he might still live for up to two or three years but, he may also die any time between then. Tonight, Mom and Dad are flying to Saudi, to see King Al-Aziz; Mom is setting up a meeting, so the King can put his weight behind us. So, my brothers and my sister, let us all come together and do everything within our power to ensure that our father is promoted to this new level. We all owe it to him for being such a generous man."

"Yes, we do," Aisha agreed, "I will keep my head low, as I always have."

"Yes, Aisha. You have only brought pride to our family," Bashir praises her. "Hope Hassan won't keep you out too late tonight?"

"No. We're pushing our date to Saturday."

"Okay, that's fine." He turned to his brothers. "Let's leave her to open the presents." They all agreed and started to head out.

"I'll follow you to school - which driver is taking you?" Kabiru asked her.

"I don't know yet but I'm leaving in about an hour."

"Cool," Kabiru said, being the last to exit, and then shut her door. She turned towards the mirror again. Aisha was relishing the thought of becoming royalty. She touched her diamond necklace, looking into the mirror, and she could already feel like a Princess.

She couldn't wait to be with John; her birthday was not complete until she had laid herself in his arms. This was the second birthday she would be spending with him. Last year was unforgettable; she spent most of the time in his room, at his uncle's house. They were all cuddled up on his bed, talking about their dreams and about the future. Back then, just ten months after meeting each other, they were so attached.

She felt so alone whenever she was not with him and being with him felt better than being cheered and praised by a thousand-other people. She went over to her wardrobe to pick out something to wear for her private party, brimming with excitement.

*****

"Oooohww!" John lamented, along with almost all the twelve people at the party, all dancing and hanging around the living room of the Lecturer's Staff Quarters, most holding plastic cups of juice and vodka. John's closest friend; Feyi, had changed the song again, from the laptop connected to the surround system.

He was just beginning to enjoy dancing Aisha, who had been here for over two hours but, within that time, he'd been making sure everyone got food and drinks, he had to go get fuel for the generator when the electricity went out, and Feyi forgot to buy the cable used to connect his Laptop to the speakers, even though he gave him the money to do so yesterday. Finally, things were going smoothly and then this?

"This song is better!" No one in the room seemed to agree with Feyi, as they all stopped dancing.

"Just get away from the laptop," John scolded, going to take over the music. Aisha held onto his fingers as he left, until their distance forced them to disconnect. She then walked over to her three friends; Ijeoma, Amina and Funke, who had been staring at her the whole time, standing at a corner of the room and holding plastic cups.

"What time is it?" Aisha asked Funke.

"...six thirty-eight."

"Where is my own drink?" She asked no one in particular.

"Take mine, birthday girl," Ijeoma said, handing Aisha her own cup.

"Thank you." Aisha collected her cup, as she turned her attention back to John at the other side of the room, fiddling with his laptop.

The music came back on and it was a dance-able song playing. Some people headed back to the center of the living room, to continue dancing. Two guys walked over together, obviously teaming up, and asked Funke and Amina to dance. The two girls smiled and then consented, before following them. Amina handed her cup to Ijeoma as she left, while Funke went with hers. Aisha and Ijeoma were then left alone.

"I thought your brother would come?" Ijeoma asked.

"I didn't tell him about the party; I didn't want anyone in my house to know - did you tell him?"

"Nope... we were chatting yesterday but we didn't talk about that."

"Ah-ah. So, you guys are now 'chatting'?" Aisha teased.

Ijeoma laughs, shyly. "Kabiru's cool."

"Whatever, it's none of my business. Just don't tell him about the party!"

"Nope, I won't."

John approached Aisha and stretched out his hands towards her. She handed her cup to Ijeoma and then collected his hands. Ijeoma was left alone, holding two cups. Aisha smiled and then started to shimmy as he led her towards the other dancing people.

John remembered when he met her at the exam hall, less than two years ago. She was so pretty, he knew he just had to find an excuse to talk to her and luckily for him there was a perfect excuse; she needed help with the exam answers. He circled all the right answers on her question paper, finished his own questions twenty minutes before the end of the exam, and then went to hang outside the hall, waiting for her to come out and hoping it would all appear unintentional when he ran into her. She finished and came looking for him, to thank him and they ended up spending over two hours together, walking around the school, from the exam hall to the Lagoon Front, and then onto the cafeteria to get some food, before her driver came to pick her, along with her brother.

Some things are just natural; things like the way they both fell in love with each other. He was eager to know everything about her, just as she was eager to know everything about him.

"Thanks for the party..." she said, as she placed her hands on his shoulders and he placed his on her waist.

"You're welcome... anything to get you to spend the day with me." She blushed. They moved along with the music.

"You should see the jewelry set my mom bought me today. It is so expensive! I wanted to come and show you but then I got scared that I might lose it in school - I'll bring it when we're alone."

"Okay."

"I was just thinking about you when I put it on," she spilled.

"Why me?"

"I... don't even know... I guess you're always on my mind."

"Not as much as you are on my mind."

"Are you sure about that?" she asked, whisked away with a bashing happiness. He didn't know how to answer the question. She just wanted to stay in his arms.

His eyes were always so honest and gentle when staring at her; she loved staring back into them. It was obvious he would do anything for her; he would even die for her. It was that same look in his eyes that made her kiss him the first time. They had been in his house for some minutes, the first time she came here to visit him, and it only took one coincidental look into her eyes, for her to lean forward and kiss him. He had that same look in his eyes as they danced.

Aisha held his gaze; pouring out all her insecurities. She knew he would never judge whatever she was feeling. She then, unconsciously, leaned forward and kissed him, while the music played on.

Ijeoma, who had been staring at the two love birds, pulled out her phone to take a picture of the precious moment, while the others in the room looked on, infected with their happiness. Aisha was in another world; one where that second lasted forever.

*****

It was seven thirty-six as Fatiu, Aisha and Kabiru's driver for the day, parked in front of the Staff Quarters where he dropped Aisha earlier.

Kabiru was in the passenger seat. "Is this the place?" he asked, threatening Fatiu.

"Yes, sir."

Kabiru stepped down, watching his balance. He was having a couple of beers at the University Guest House, with his friends, when he saw Ijeoma's social media update. She posted a picture of Aisha kissing that guy; the same one he always saw her with, whenever he went to pick her. He was just wondering what girl he would message to come hang out with him, scrolling through his phone, when he saw Ijeoma's post. She then wrote; 'I pray for a love like this' beneath the picture.

He entered the compound, uninterested in asking questions. He saw two guys and two girls outside, having a conversation, holding red plastic cups. He ignored them and went inside, following the sound of the music.

He entered the living room of John's uncle's house, looking around for Aisha. Ijeoma spotted him and walked over to him, smiling.

"Hey! What are you doing here?" she asked, as she got to him.

"Why the fuck would you put that picture of my sister on your profile?!" he yelled at her, with violence in his eyes.

Ijeoma was shocked. "I'm... sorry. I didn't know you would see it."

"So, this is the rubbish you both do around campus?"

"No –"

"Where is she?!" he barked.

"She's upstairs."

"Upstairs doing what?"

"I don't know - she's with John."

"The same person she was kissing?" Kabiru asked, infuriated. Everyone in the party had turned their attention to him. They all looked on, alarmed.

Kabiru disregarded Ijeoma who was hesitating to answer. He found the staircase and climbed upstairs.

He yanked open the first door he saw but found no one was there. He then went across the hallway and twisted open the next door know but it was locked.

"Aisha!" he yelled.

Aisha was shocked to hear Kabiru's voice; of all the voices to hear, now that she was making out with John. John was startled at the tone of the voice also. "Yes?" Aisha replied.

"Open this door, now!"

She quickly buttoned up her pink corporate shirt and clasped her black jeans. She then hurried towards the door, setting her Hijab in place, while John also sat up on the bed, trying to look casual.

"What the hell do you think you're doing?!" he screamed at her as she opened the door, not even taking a glance at John. He then grabbed her by the arm and dragged her out, heading towards the stairs. John was irritated by the way Kabiru rough-handled her. He got off the bed and followed them.

"Take it easy," he said, frantically. Aisha shot him a look, telling him to be calm.

Kabiru pulled her downstairs to the living room before letting go of her. He then walked over to Ijeoma, who was looking on at the scene with the rest of the people at the party.

"Take that picture off your profile and delete it from your phone now!" Kabiru commanded her. She quickly pulled out her phone and did as he said. He stood by waiting for her to finish.

"I've done it."

He then stormed back towards Aisha, who was just about to break into tears. He grabbed her by the hand and continued to drag her, heading outside the house. John couldn't take the harshness anymore.

"Don't treat her like that. She's done nothing wrong!" he yelled, in her defense.

Kabiru let go of her and marched towards him. "You bastard! You think my sister is your play-thing?!"

Feyi, and two other friends of John, sensed the impending violence. They both rushed to stand in between Kabiru and John. "Look, behave yourself and get out of here! Where do you think you are?" Feyi, growled, ready to tear Kabiru apart. "Carry your sister and get the hell out of our party!"

Kabiru realized that he was outnumbered. He gave a final look to John, warning him. He then grabbed Aisha and continued to drag her out. He pulled her out of the house while she cried, looking down at the floor, ashamed. John followed them outside, wishing he could stop what was happening.

Aisha then reacted, rebelling. "Stop dragging me!" she protested. He looked at her, judgmentally.

"Are you complaining? Your mother and father would hear all about this rubbish - I still have the picture on my phone."

"Do your worst!" she yelled back. She then walked outside the compound by herself, towards the parked car. Kabiru took one more threatening look at John and his friends before following his sister out.

John watched Aisha leave unaware that this was the last time he was going see her in over seven years.

*****

Aisha and John walk towards the car park of the Church of Assumption, in Ikoyi. He has both his hands crossed together, just below his waist. She has both hands dipped into the back pockets of her jeans.

She had stayed till it was past seven p.m. because she saw how genuinely busy John got, with so many people seeking his attention, but she wasn't going to leave without having this quiet moment with him.

"So, I heard... emmm... Archbishop Alexander, talking about donations for a charity project?" she puts in.

"Yes, that's right. I'm actually in charge of the project; we're trying to open feeding centers in some parts of the city, so we can give free breakfast and dinner to the hungry."

"Wow... it sounds so nice; so honestly charitable... I want to be a part of it."

"Okay..." John says, observing her sincerity.

"I was thinking of donating some money to that and maybe help with the field work - when I have the time - is that okay?"

"Really?"

"Yes... if it's okay with you?" she asks.

"Of course, it is. Why wouldn't it be?

She giggles. "I don't know... maybe you don't want to be around me much." He is slightly taken aback but tries to hide it, by saying nothing. "I know," she continues, looking towards his face, hoping to catch his eyes, "...I betrayed you."

John realizes it's becoming impossible to avoid the obvious. "You didn't betray me, Aisha –"

"Yes, I did, John..." she argues, "I didn't try to make it work; I ran away and I wasn't even bold enough to confront you, to explain."

"The situation must have been beyond your control."

"Was it?" She finally connects with his eyes. She sees the same honesty and gentleness in them. "I'm older now and looking back on it all, I know we could have made it work, if only I was strong enough to stick with you," she pours out, with her eyes feeling moist.

John is uncomfortable revisiting those thoughts. "It all worked out for the best," he says, smiling appropriately, "we both ended up quite well."

She smiles back, appropriately too, gathering her crashing emotions. "Yes, we did."

They get to her car, where Nuru and Abu are waiting. She had told them to go ahead of her before she left the crowd at the Bazaar. Nuru starts the car and Abu gets into the front passenger seat as she gets to them. John stands by her as she opens the back door.

"It was nice seeing you... again," she says, looking up at him. He was always taller than her.

"It was nice seeing you too, Aisha."

"Can I... hug you?" she asks tentatively.

He stretches out his arms, smiling, inviting her. "Of course."

She wraps her hands around him and he does the same. She is then about to let go but her arms refuse to let her. She always loved his embrace and she still does. John holds the embrace, waiting for her to be ready to let go. She heaves and sniffs.

Aisha finally lets go of him and he sees a tear rolling down her right eye. She quickly wipes it off, trying unsuccessfully to hide it.

"Bye," she says before getting into the car and shutting the door.

John doesn't know what to think of the tear. He is reminded of how deep their love was.

She looks up at him through her wound-up windows, with melancholy in her eyes, as Nuru drives out of the car park.

He waves at her, wishing he didn't have to live without her.

CHAPTER 4

Sunday morning has always been a great time for Hassan and his friends to play an exhilarating game of Polo, at the Ikoyi Polo club. Ever since he relocated to Abuja, he's realized how much he misses Sunday mornings, like this one. He got into Lagos this Monday, with plans to stay for three weeks, and since then he'd been eagerly looking forward to Sunday because of the polo game, and also because he gets to have his fiancé; Aisha, to himself for the whole day.

Hassan hurriedly pulls up his white, denim playing trousers, over his boxers. He then throws on his Ralph Lauren polo shirt and tucks it into his pants.

He takes out his leather belt and buckles it over his waist. He then places his feet into his knee-length polo boots before zipping them up.

Time to play some Polo. He puts on his equestrian helmet and then dips his clothes into his own locker, before locking it with a padlock. He picks up his mallet, leaning on the locker beside him and the heads outside the changing room.

He got here later than his three friends, who had all to come to play on the same four-man team, against the Ikoyi Polo Club horse grooms. In his twelve years of playing Polo against the horse grooms, his team has only won six times.

Back when he was just fourteen years old, he would come and play with his Uncle Fayeed; his father's youngest brother, who was about twenty-eight at the time, and his friends, against the horse grooms. They always got a thrashing from the young men who had spent most of their lives amidst horses and the young men always got an ego boost from humbling their employers; a tradition that the predecessors did not forget to pass on to their successors at the horse stables of the Ikoyi Polo Club. The first time they won, when Hassan was sixteen, his Uncle; Fayeed, turned the Polo Club bar into a party floor. They danced, spraying champagne on all their female guests, who had come to cheer for them; they ordered more chicken barbecue than they could eat and they kept ordering more and more drinks from the bar. That was also the first day Hassan got drunk on Alcohol and misbehaved pretty badly. In his drunkenness, he decided it was a good idea to kiss one of his Uncle's friend's Fiance. The young lady laughed it off but his Uncle's friend didn't take it so lightly. If not for Fayeed's timely intervention, Hassan would have gotten his adolescent face pummeled in.

Major Hassan Ibrahim emerges onto the polo field, where his friends; Rasheed, Jamiu and Danjuma are already warming up their horses. They trot around the horse racetrack, surrounding the polo field, trying not to wear the horses down before the game. The four caretakers have also mounted their horses and are within the polo field, knocking the plastic ball back and forth, with their long-handled wooden mallets.

"Finally... can we play?" Jamiu sneers. The other men on the field look towards Hassan as he approaches his horse, which is being held by a younger groom, who's not playing today.

"Yes, we can!" Hassan exclaims, excited. He collects the horse whip from the young caretaker and mounts his horse smoothly. He holds his mallet in his right and uses his left hand to hold both the reins and the whip. He then nudges the horse gently with his heels and rides onto the racetrack to join his teammates, feeling the rocking of his leather saddle.

"Time to get our asses kicked," Rasheed mocks, as the four men converge, with their horses.

"No talking like that! It is that same defeatist attitude that makes them beat you every time," Danjuma scolds.

"No matter what we say, they're going to beat us; stop fooling yourself," Rasheed resounds, not feeling the flames of war within his veins, like Hassan and Danjuma, who are both in the military.

"Let us just play!" Jamiu yells, impatiently.

"We are going to win today. We can't go into the game, planning to lose, Rasheed," Hassan says, motivating his team, "...and Jamiu, 'playing' is all about winning or losing. Even if they are going to beat us again, we should at least put up a good fight."

"Exactly. We're not just going to lie dead on the ground," Danjuma contributes.

"Yes, Major Hassan. We are going to win... after we break our Mallets on their heads, right?" Rasheed jibes further. Jamiu laughs and Danjuma chuckles. Hassan gives Rasheed an angry look. He replies him with a defiant look.

Rasheed is the second son of Chief Aregbesola; one of Nigeria's richest business moguls, and has been Hassan's friend since they were in secondary school; longer than Jamiu or Danjuma. They've both always had a way of countering each other's opinions, which used to lead to numerous physical fights when they were younger, but as they've grown older, they've learnt to restrict their fighting to words and angry looks. Still, when it comes down to it, Hassan still values the opinion of Rasheed over Danjuma, who is his subordinate in the Nigerian Army and over Jamiu, who works for his father; General Ibrahim.

"Me, I am going to play. You guys should join me." Jamiu says, riding off into the polo field. The others watch him leave.

"If we lose today, I'll know it's your fault," Hassan says to Rasheed, before whipping his horse and riding off into the polo field also. Rasheed laughs, drunkenly.

"No problem!" Rasheed yells to him. He then turns to Danjuma. "He will always need someone to blame after, for his battered ego." Danjuma chuckles courteously in return and then rides off. Rasheed whips his horse violently and gallops towards his teammates. "Oya now! Let's do this!"

The four grooms converge, ready to begin the first Chukka of the game.

*****

Nuru drives Aisha out of Lekki phase-one and towards Awolowo road, in Ikoyi. Abu is also seated at the front passenger seat, while Aisha is seated in the owner's corner. Nuru slows down as they get to the toll gates, leading to Victoria Island, and pulls out his credited pass-card. He swipes the card in front of the card reader and the toll gates automatically go up, granting them passage. He sticks his hand back in, winds up the window and drives on.

Last night was a turning point for Aisha. She couldn't hold back the tears that streamed down her face, all the way from the Church of Assumption in Ikoyi, when she left John, to her house in Lekki phase-one. She hadn't had any reason to cry like that since the night of her nineteenth birthday. Then, Kabiru had dragged her back home, against her desires, away from the private party John had put together for her, and for some reason Kabiru never reported her to their Parents, or even to their senior brothers; he kept it as their secret, but that night she locked herself in her room and cried till the appearance of the morning light. She didn't reply John's messages or pick his calls; she never did after that day. At her young age, she was forced to make the hard choice of helping her father or helping herself and she chose to stick by her father's side; she chose to stay away from John, to avoid anything like what happened at the party, that would bring shame to her father's name and hinder him from becoming the Emir.

Last night, she was reminded of all the tears she shed that night, over four years ago, and it caused a new stream of tears to flow, as she was driven away from John. Back then, she sacrificed her happiness for her father but why is she doing the same thing now? Alhaji Mustapha is already the Emir of Kano but Aisha's still missing her own happiness. It seems as though it's too late but if it isn't, should she take the chance; should she reach for him? Would John reach back?

Nuru drives the black Mercedes S class onto the Ikoyi bridge. Aisha is conscious of the fact that they will pass by the Church of Assumption, on their way to the Ikoyi Polo Club. She imagines herself catching a faint glimpse of John as they pass by but she knows it's highly unlikely. It's a Sunday morning, there would be a lot of people at the church and John would probably be performing some duties within the building. She misses him but after their last meeting there was no opening for another encounter. They didn't exchange numbers and they didn't make any future appointments. However, Aisha remembers Archbishop Alexander, at the Bazaar, talking about a charity project, to feed the hungry across the state. She had filled a small form with details of her name, phone number and the amount she was pledging to the charity cause. John even said that he is in charge of the project, so it might just be the best way to reach out to him.

She opens her handbag, lying beside her, and pulls out the piece of paper with the account number for the charity project, as Nuru drives down the Ikoyi bridge.

They swing by the church and Aisha can't help but look into the compound, to see if she would catch a glimpse of John. She doesn't.

She pulls up her mobile phone and goes ahead to make a transfer of one million Naira to the account number, just as she had written in her pledge. She had also volunteered to help with the field work, distributing the food at the designated centers, so one way or the other, she would be seeing John soon. Last night, she realized how unhappy she is, even though she is surrounded by so much luxury. She saw a vision in her mind, of being trapped in a house with Hassan for the rest of her life. In the vision, the house was expensively furnished and she was adorned with precious jewelry but her heart was hollow; she felt a void in her chest. She was being suffocated with the odor of the fresh leather furniture and the freshly painted walls and she just wanted a breath of fresh air; she just wanted John. She knows he is the only one who can fill her void and she feels so sad for Hassan because he will never understand.

Nuru drives into the Ikoyi Polo club. It's eleven, forty-five in the morning. He drives towards the car park. Aisha sees Hassan walking towards his green Mercedes G class, along with his friends Rasheed, Jamiu and another.

They must have finished the game, much to Aisha's relief. She doesn't find Polo that amazing but Hassan obviously does. Abu points towards Hassan and Nuru drives towards them.

Hassan looks towards the black Mercedes approaching and immediately knows it's Aisha. He smiles as the car comes to a halt beside him. Aisha steps down, holding her handbag, wearing a stylish sky-blue Abaya, which is tied with a white ribbon at the waist, and her head covered with a sparkling white Hijab, wound down around her neck. Hassan beams with pride as he sees her. Nuru drives on to find a parking space.

"My love," Hassan says.

"My love," she replies. They hold hands.

"Ah-ah!" Rasheed exclaims, "Aisha-Aisha... you look so delicious and nutritious. Like a fresh banana... I'm sure Hassan can wait to peel you open, one by one." She springs into laughter, so does Hassan and the other two.

"My friend, go and face your wife at home and leave my own for me!" Hassan retorts, comically. Rasheed laughs.

"How are you Rasheed and how is Binta?" she enquires.

"We are both fine, dear."

"Hi, Jamiu," she greets.

"Hi Aisha. You look lovely," Jamiu says, slightly bowing, courteously.

"Thanks... I haven't met you yet," she says, turning to Danjuma.

"Hi, I'm Danjuma. I'm a Captain under the Major."

"We work together, dear," Hassan cuts in.

"So, how was the match?" Aisha asks Hassan.

Rasheed jumps in. "They thwacked us nine-two." He then laughs, purposely trying to infuriate Hassan. Aisha chuckles.

"You'll beat them next time," she says to Hassan.

"It's people like you that keep feeding his head with all this nonsense, that's why he comes here every Sunday expecting to win," Rasheed mocks.

"We're going to New Yorkers for breakfast, have you eaten?" Hassan asks her, ignoring Rasheed.

"Not really, just had Tea; I can eat," Aisha replies.

"Me, I have to get going, though," Jamiu injects.

"Me too; I made some plans," Danjuma adds.

"No problem. See you guys later," Hassan says. They shake hands with Rasheed and leave but not before giving a courteous bow to Aisha.

Hassan lets go of Aisha's hand and walks over to the Driver's side of his green Mercedes SUV. She also walks over to the Passenger side. Rasheed's flashy looking BMW i-8 is parked just beside. He pushes a button on his remote Key, knowingly, and the headlights flash, while the car twerps.

"Is this your car?" Aisha asks, amused.

"Yes, it is!" Rasheed brags, "just got it last week, even though I ordered it from Germany six months ago. It runs on electricity and a little bit of fuel."

"Wow... an electric car? So, you care about the ozone layer?" she asks, sarcastically.

"Of course, I do!" Rasheed exclaims, comically, "I am appalled about to climate change! ...meanwhile, I have a better idea than New Yorkers for breakfast. We just hired one bad-ass Chef like this, that has been wowing me at every meal - he is really good; I am always looking forward to what he'll cook next - let's go to my house, hang out with my wife, while my Chef cooks us a wonderful breakfast... or rather Brunch." Aisha looks towards Hassan, to see if he consents. "Plus, you get to save your New Yorker's money," Rasheed persuades.

"Cheapskate!" Hassan jibes.

"See my car and see your car; who is the cheapskate amongst us?" Rasheed jibes, taking that as a 'yes' and heading towards the driver's door of his car.

Hassan laughs. "Nice ride, bro... but I will still beat you to your house."

Rasheed laughs, maniacally. "In your dreams! This car is a bullet! You can never get to Banana Island before me." He lifts open the swan-doors of his sports car and sits inside.

"Oya na... it's today you'll know that Superman is faster than a bullet."

"It seems you need another dent in your ego. The beating you got on the field was not enough - oya na!"

Rasheed pulls down his doors and starts his car. Hassan starts his car also.

"Put on your seat belt," Hassan says to her, with his battle-face on, as he also does the same.

"Hassan," she gently protests, "please be careful."

"I have been trained extensively in military evasive driving; trust me, I can handle this."

"Okay," she resigns, knowing better than to try and stop him. "Bismillah...Tawakkalna ala Allah," she whispers out loud, which means: In the name of Allah... I place my absolute trust on Allah.

*****

"I think we should call her now..." Deacon Benedict argues, with Father John. "First, to confirm if this is her pledge and also to thank her. It's not every day we get a million-naira donation; this is the biggest donation to the Feed-Lagos project yet."

John listens and it's obvious there is no way to avoid this. He is the head of the Feed-Lagos project and he will be the one speaking to her, to thank her for her generous donation. He watched her leave yesterday evening and after that he prayed that she would just disappear, the same way she did over four years ago. Doesn't she realize that she is not making it any easier to move on by coming around him? What is her plan? It took him four years of faithfulness and dedication to purity, to help him pick together the pieces of his broken heart. She smashed his heart on the floor when she turned and walked out of his life; when she purposely erased him from all the existents in her universe. She locked the doors to her warmth and shut him out, to the cold streets of pain. She owes it to him to stay away; doesn't she know that?

"She also volunteered for the field work," Benedict adds, "she left her number in the form we passed out; I have it on my laptop," he says, scrolling through his laptop, lying on the table in Father's John's office. John is behind his desk, trying to feel from the Spirit, what this set of incidences mean and what will come out of it all.

"Get her on the line, so I can thank her," John decides.

"Okay, Father," Benedict says.

He pulls Miss Aisha Mustapha's number from his laptop and dials it on the church phone.

*****

Aisha is seated beside Binta; Rasheed's wife, at the poolside of their home, in Banana Island. It's six-thirty in the evening and they are having fruity cocktails, while discussing details about where Aisha buys some of her designer Hijabs and all the various styles of tying the Hijab that Binta never knew.

The two guys, Rasheed and Hassan, have moved their competitive spirits over to the snooker table, just underneath a shed beside the swimming pool, to continue deciding who is better than who, while they smoke their cigarettes, away from the ladies.

"If I was you, I would just drown myself in this pool right now!" Rasheed exclaims, "I have beaten you six times in a row and you still want more. Are you Rocky Balboa?! In addition to the beating you got at the polo field?"

"You mean 'we got'... and I won the car race," Hassan states, unperturbed.

"I mean 'you' — I went to the polo field ready to lose, as usual, so I basically just had fun, while you lost because you were expecting to win... and as for the car race, you only won because you're suicidal; I still wanted to hold my wife and not die on Bourdillon road."

"Either way, you lost."

"Aisha, how did you survive that driving?" Rasheed yells out to her.

"Haaa... Allah protected us! Hassan is 'trained in military evasive driving'," she sings the last words. Binta and Rasheed laugh. Hassan has on an indifferent look, while Rasheed is racking up a new game of Snooker.

Aisha's phone rings, cutting through the laughs. She pulls it out of her bag, while Hassan observes her. She doesn't have the ID of the caller, so she goes ahead to pick it up.

"Hello Miss Mustapha, this is Deacon Benedict, from the Church of Assumption, Ikoyi," the voice comes over the phone.

"Hi."

"We would like to confirm if you sent us the sum of one million for the Feed-Lagos project?"

"Yes, I did," Aisha replies.

"We are truly grateful, please hold on for Father John, who would like to thank you personally." Her heart skips a beat. She looks over and sees Hassan's eyes on her.

She gets up from the poolside seat. "Let me take this inside," she says to Binta, placing her hand over the phone's mouthpiece and ignoring Hassan's look. She heads inside the house.

"Hello, Miss Mustapha," John says, collecting the phone.

"Hello... John," she says as she gets to the glass door, leading into the house. She pushes it open and walks in.

"I would really like to thank you for your generous donation to the Feed-Lagos project," John starts, "with help like this we can make this dream a reality; getting a basic human necessity like food, to thousands of people in Lagos, on a regular basis."

"I think it's a great initiative and I am in full support of the idea. You can count on me to support this fully and I will be available regularly, to help with the distribution of the food."

"That is even more generous of you. We look forward to kickstarting the project, early next month -

"Can I see you – can we meet?" she suddenly asks, cutting him short. She couldn't bear the formal talk anymore.

John has made up his mind to handle any interaction with her appropriately. There are many people looking up to him and he cannot give into his carnal desires, no matter how tempting. "Of course, we can... at the church office."

"That's fine. Tomorrow morning?"

"Emmm... sure."

"Okay. I'll swing by at eleven a.m."

"That's just fine. Thank you once again, Miss Mustapha."

"...bye." She puts down the phone, slightly satisfied that she will be seeing John tomorrow. Still, from his tone, she can tell he is focused on keeping things casual between them. Has he completely turned off all his feelings for her? She knows she deserves that and even worse for what she did but she is still holding onto a string of hope; that somehow, he can forgive her sins and look at her with eyes of unbridled love once more. She will bear her heart out to him tomorrow and she prays Allah will grant this wish, if it is not Haram.

She heads back outside to join Hassan, Rasheed and Binta. She takes a deep breath, regains her composure and pulls open the glass door, leading to the poolside of Rasheed's home.

CHAPTER 5

Aisha heads back outside to join Hassan, Rasheed and Binta. She takes a deep breath, regains her composure and pulls open the glass doors leading to the poolside of Rasheed's home. She walks over to Binta and takes her seat, before putting her phone back in her bag.

Hassan kept his eyes on her, from the point she opened the glass door. Somehow, he has never been able to tell what is on the mind of his bride-to-be, who has been betrothed to him for over ten years now. All he sees when he looks at her is the innocent virgin but somehow, he suspects that no one could be this innocent. She is supposed to be his but somehow, he feels she is out of his reach.

He remembers the day her father, now the Sultan of Kano, announced to his father that he would want to join their families, by betrothing Aisha to Hassan. Both men had been long-time friends and General Ibrahim always went to extra miles to see that Alhaji Mustapha was protected, and he continues to do the same now that he is Emir. Hassan, that day, remembers being so excited that the beautiful Aisha sitting across the room, who all the boys had been crushing on, even though she was just sixteen, would be his bride. He felt like the alpha-male but he also remembers looking into her eyes, across the distance of the room, and seeing that she was not happy; she was just shocked. He felt he could woo her and get her eating from his palms in no time but ten years later, he can still feel the distance between them. He wishes she could fall in love with him; just close her eyes and fall into his arms but she hasn't yet, and he is scared that she never will. Yes, he wants her; who wouldn't want such a resplendent creature? In the end, he will do his best to keep her, like his father had commanded.

The glass doors leading to the house open and Chef Kenneth steps onto the backyard. "Dinner is ready, sir."

"Thank you, Kenneth," Rasheed retorts. He then turns to Hassan. So, you tasted this guy's brunch, now it's time to taste his dinner – I wonder what new style he has come up with this evening!"

"If his dinner is anything better than that brunch I ate, I might just steal him from you. Can't you see how patiently I have been waiting for this meal?"

Rasheed laughs, as they head toward the two ladies. "My Chef is off limits; if you miss his food you can always swing by."

"Hmmm... that's still reasonable."

Aisha and Binta get up from the straw chairs and prepare to join them. Aisha picks her handbag and waits for Hassan to get beside her. She then holds his hand and pulls on it, forcing him to stop while the other two head inside. "I can't stay for dinner," she tells him.

"Why not?"

"I have a board meeting in the morning and… some other meetings I need to prepare for."

"But I already called Abu and told him to get your car home. Just stay for dinner and then I'll drop you."

"And he did that without confirming with me?" she asks, taken aback.

"Relax, Abu is a trained and skilled guard; he knew you were in good hands. If you insist, I'll drop you back at home right now."

"…please do."

"Okay, let's leave." He holds onto her palm and they walk into the house, through the glass door. Rasheed has gone to take a seat on the dinner table, while the chef displays and explains the food to him. Binta seems to have gone upstairs.

Aisha knows that she must say a proper goodbye before leaving, even though she is in a hurry to be alone right now. Ever since the phone call with John, some minutes ago, she began to feel like she was living a lie. She knows that, at the end of the day, she wants to be happy but the path she is heading on is not taking her there. She thought she could recreate a version of what she felt with John, seven-plus years ago, with Hassan, but now she realizes she was utterly wrong. The only escape out of this unwanted reality is to take a chance and reach out for John.

Ever since that phone call, she realized how desperate she is for a life happiness and how this could be her last chance. Oh, let her heart not be cast into eternal sadness.

"I wish I could stay but Aisha needs to get home," Hassan announces.

"Awww... so sad. You're going to miss this wonderful dinner," Rasheed taunts, licking his spoon after having a taste of the sauce presented to him by Chef Kenneth. Aisha and Hassan laugh. "...but no worries, Kenneth will pack some take away for you both... and Binta and I have something to tell you; we were hoping to do it after dinner."

"What's that?" Hassan asks. Aisha is curious too.

"Binta! Please come down, dear."

"Okay, dear!" She resounds. The door to the master bedroom upstairs is shut and Binta makes her way down the stairs. She sees Aisha and Hassan, standing. "Are you leaving?" Binta asks Aisha.

"Yes, I am. Sorry, I can't stay," Aisha replies, with a guilty smile. Rasheed gets up and goes to stand beside Binta, as she gets downstairs. He then puts his hand around her waist.

"It's okay," Binta says before taking a look at her husband. "...we were going to tell you later but... well... we're expecting our first child. I'm three months pregnant!"

"Oh, that's so beautiful! ...I had a feeling that you were pregnant, the way you've been carrying yourself, so daintily, but I didn't want to jump into conclusions – I'm so happy for you!" Aisha spurts.

"This irresponsible man is about to become a father?!" Hassan exclaims.

"You're very stupid! ...and yes, I'm about to be a Papa."

"I am happy for you, brother."

"Thanks, Hassan. Na you remain now o!" Rasheed taunts.

Aisha and Hassan laugh shyly. "One day, very soon," Hassan replies. Chef Kenneth returns from the kitchen with two nylon bags, containing two plastic bowls each.

"I packed it separately, so you have the same thing in both bags, sir," Kenneth says to Hassan.

"Thank you," he returns, collecting the nylon bags from Kenneth.

"I'll try and come by this week, so we can talk," Aisha says to Binta.

"That'll be great. I'm usually bored."

"Wednesday," Aisha sets, as she and Hassan turn towards the front door of the house.

"I'll be expecting you," replies Binta, as she and Rasheed follow them behind.

Hassan had parked his green Mercedes G class inside the lovely compound of Rasheed's Banana Island home. It's just about seven thirty in the evening and the sky's golden glow is being replaced with the darkness of the night.

They step out onto the front of the house, which has a well-manicured lawn, with glowing yellow lamps planted in it. Marble floors lead from the front door to the driveway, where the cars are parked.

"See you later, bro," Hassan says to Rasheed, as he pushes the remote key, to unlock the car.

Aisha walks over to Binta and gives her a gentle hug. "Take care of yourself."

"I will, dear. Thanks," Binta replies, smiling as they let go of each other. Aisha then walks over to the front passenger side of the green SUV.

Hassan and Rasheed shake hands and Hassan gets into his car. Aisha gets in also. Rasheed and Binta head back inside the house, while Hassan starts his car.

Aisha puts on her seat belt waiting for Hassan to drive out but instead he reaches forth and holds her palm. She looks him in the eyes and notices he's been staring at her. He leans forward to kiss her and her heart leaps out of her chest; the last thing she wants at this moment.

She heaves as he approaches her lips. She then gently places her hand on his chest, resisting him. "Please... I don't want that right now... I have a lot on my mind."

Hassan's ego is shattered. He almost turns angry but comes to remembrance of the fact that she is not just any girl to him. She is the daughter of the Emir; she is his bride-to-be. "I love you, Aisha... I don't know if I say that enough but I really do... I want you to fall in love with me too... and I know you have not yet."

Aisha looks him in the eyes, wishing she could refute what he just said but, somehow, it must have become obvious that she doesn't love him and she wasn't brought up to lie. "Hassan..." she starts a sentence but doesn't finish.

"All you need to do is give me a chance to win your heart. Tell me what you need me to change and I'll do it. I don't want to lose you, Aisha. I want to marry you."

She still has nothing to say. How can she explain to him that there is nothing he can do? Hassan doesn't expect an instant reply.

"We haven't made plans for our official engagement yet, talk more our marriage," he continues, "don't you think it's about time we started making constructive plans?"

"I... I will put it in mind," she musters.

He realizes he is pressuring her and decides to ease off. He turns the car around and drives out of the compound.

*****

It's three a.m. and it's time for the Lauds; also known as the Morning Prayer. Members of the Clergy make their way into the church, while the city of Lagos sleeps. On his way to becoming a Priest, Father John had to learn and understand the official public prayer life of the Catholic church. This consists of the Liturgy of Hours and the Mass. The Liturgy of Hours is the official set of prayers, said at various hours of the day, to sanctify that day with prayer. It takes place every three hours, starting from midnight, onto nine pm. Members of the Priesthood, including deacons aspiring to become Priests, find it mandatory to observe the Liturgy of Hours. Back when John was still in the monastery, his entire day was centered around the Liturgy of Hours.

John sees a vision in his mind, of Aisha stretching her hand out to him, before snapping back to reality. He then opens the Morning Prayer with a Versicle from the book of Psalms. There are about ten people in the room, at this early hour of the morning; the Parish Priest, the assistant Parish Priest and a few deacons. John is the third Priest in the Church of Assumption and he is also third in hierarchy.

He sings aloud the Versicle and the small congregation sings back the response.

*****

It's five, fifty-six, as the Muezzin in the Mustapha's Lagos compound sings out the second call to the Fajr prayer. Aisha just steps out her bathroom, having finished her Ablution. She goes over to pull out her prayer mat and lays it on the clean floor, facing the Qibla. She then steps on the mat and opens her heart's intentions to Allah before starting her prayer.

She thanks Allah for the new day and asks for guidance as she plans to take a chance on love, today. She thinks about her parents and siblings and hopes they will support her decision to do something so different from what they are expecting. She looks into her mind and sees John's gentle face, staring back at her, and she almost reaches out to touch him.

She raises both her palms to her ears and utters, in Arabic; "Allah is the greatest." She then places her left hand over her belly and places her right hand over it, before reciting the opening prayer; "subhanakal-lahumma…."

*****

Father Richard, the assistant Parish Priest, conducted the morning Mass, which started at six-thirty a.m. Only a few members of the Laity attend the morning Mass on a Monday, such as this, but all members of the Parish Clergy are mandated to. Father John would like to say that he was concentrating all through the Mass but it would not be true. He has been distracted and troubled by thoughts of Aisha, since midnight. He can feel a great force charging towards him and he is not yet prepared to resist that force. The gates to his heart are about to be broken open, even though he is trying desperately to hold them closed.

"Good morning, Father John," a young lady says, who attended the morning Mass.

"Good morning, my dear," Father John replies, recognizing the young lady.

"Please, I would like to make a confession... I hope you have the time?"

"Of course. I always encourage all, to make confessions as frequently as possible. I'll meet you in the confession booth."

"Thank you, Father."

She walks towards the confession booth, examining her conscience. She tells God, in her heart, that she is truly sorry for her sins and she makes a strong resolution not to sin again. She enters the confession booth, shuts the door and sits down.

Shortly, Father John joins her. He blesses her and then she makes the sign of the cross, before saying; "bless me Father, for I have sinned..."

*****

Aisha made the ten-a.m. meeting at her office, with their media agency, to discuss the latest marketing campaign for Vodasat Telecom's new custom smart phone.

Being the head of business development for the company, she had to be in the room, to give approval of the strategies that were going to be used to launch the latest arm of her father's business. Alhaji Mustapha is widely known to be the owner of Vodasat Telecoms but in truth, he only owns thirty percent of the shares, after he sold a large percentage to international investors.

Usman, one of her older brothers, is also in the room, being the head of marketing. He has been throwing questions at the gentleman standing behind the screen, trying a little too hard to distract everyone with his visual effects. All Aisha has been able to think of is the fact that it's just thirty minutes to eleven a.m., when she has scheduled to meet with John. She has been framing her words and testing them on an imaginary John, trying to predict his reactions.

"Thank you, Akindele," says Usman to the gentleman presenting, "we would push forward with week one of your strategy and have another meeting next week Friday, to assess the efficacy."

"Thank you, Mr Usman," Akindele says, before gathering his technical equipment. Usman stands from his chair and so does almost-every one of the fifteen-people seated in the room. He walks over to Aisha, who has a wistful look on her face, still glued to her chair.

"Hi sis. How did you find the presentation?" Usman asks Aisha, leaning over her lovingly.

"It was... really good. If they can create the kind of engagement they're talking about, the product should do the rest."

"Yeah, I think so too. It's a good choice we made, going with this media agency, this year."

"It seems so."

"So, are you ready for the meeting with the board members?" Usman asks, all revved up.

"I... was hoping you could handle that alone? You know you usually do all the talking anyway - I have to see a friend, urgently... I'll be back by noon," she requests a favor.

"The meeting will be finished by then — it's fine. Hope your friend is fine?

"Yes... he is."

"He? ...none of my business. Just be careful." Usman pats her on the shoulder and heads out of the meeting room.

Aisha looks around and sees that she is alone in the room, with the large conference table and empty chairs. She takes a deep breath and resolves against her cold feet. She picks up her handbag and leaves.

*****

Father John is in his office, working on a schedule for the Feed-Lagos charity project, trying to distract himself from the fact that Aisha is going to walk in through his door any minute.

Certainly, he will keep his calm and hear what she says. Hopefully, he will not be moved to make a cataclysmic decision, no matter how much he wants to rekindle the past. He is a member of the Priesthood now and his life belongs to Someone greater than himself. He cannot compromise for self-satisfaction; this is what he has been telling himself but he still fears the force that is charging toward his gates.

A knock on the door. "...come in," John replies, feigning confidence. Deacon Benedict opens the door and steps in.

"Miss Aisha Mustapha is here to see you, Father."

"Okay. Let her in."

"Yes, Father." Benedict opens the door and signals for Aisha to approach. She soon appears at the door, wearing a white long dress, with long sleeves, wrapped with a purple cape, and held around the waist with a red ribbon, and wearing a purple Hijab. Benedict steps aside as she walks in, clutching her handbag and staring at John. She takes a seat at the opposite side of his desk and places her handbag on the floor. Benedict shuts the door and leaves.

"Hi," Aisha says, breathing out.

"Hi... Aisha."

She is about to start her well-constructed speech but then she sees those eyes again and she doesn't feel like an outsider. She doesn't feel that she needs to properly explain herself or come up with persuasive words, so she smiles.

He has been keeping her gaze too, as though waiting for his judgment. He has no idea what to say until she speaks. Finally, she does.

"Is it... too late?"

"Too late... for what?" John asks, struggling to understand.

"For our love story."

CHAPTER 6

Taking a stroll through the verdant campus streets with Aisha always felt so extraordinary to John. It was some minutes after five p.m. and the sun in the sky above was just turning golden, while the breeze rustling through the tree leaves was getting cooler. John and Aisha had taken another long stroll through the campus, like they had been doing frequently, since they met at the exam hall, about six months ago. He had come to meet her in her classroom, over an hour ago. He knew by now that she always finished classes by four p.m. on Thursdays.

After leaving her classroom, they first stopped to get food at the cafeteria, then they passed by the sport's complex to stare wistfully at the people playing soccer and basketball, while they carried on their endless conversations. It was then that John, for the first time, invited her to come over to his uncle's staff quarters on campus, where he stayed. Aisha agreed, so they then continued their stroll towards the staff quarters.

Aisha already knew that John stayed on campus with his uncle, Professor Amaechi; a senior lecturer in the Department of Philosophy. She had been getting closer to John, for six months, but he had never once tried to get her alone, in a private place. They would usually just walk around the school, whenever they met, until her driver came to pick her up, along with her brother; Kabiru. They'd ended up telling each other so much about themselves and it brought them closer together.

It was easy talking to John and it was fun too; he always had such interesting views about every topic and he was always ready to explore every idea down its roots. To be honest, she had wanted him to ask her over to his place for over a month now but she can't really tell why. Maybe she too wanted to be alone with him, in a private place.

"...as far as I'm concerned, cars are just 'local' inventions," John continued, as they got closer to his house. Aisha was amused by the friendly argument they were having; she was smiling through her purple Hijab and clutching her black handbag in her left hand, as they walked down the road.

"So, because you can't drive a car across the continent, it's useless?" she asked, inciting him further. John was brimming with energy, like he'd just had too many cups of coffee. He got in front of her, walking backwards, as he passionately made his point.

"Yes! I mean, imagine, you buy a car and the only place it can take you is across Nigeria – which is even dangerous because of the long distances – so all you do is drive it around your city or state. That makes it a local invention to me. I mean, the World is now a global village and we all need to reach outside our countries to do something great with ourselves but as it turns out, you can't take your car to the UK, SA or the US; you must leave it behind in Lagos, like some piece of furniture in your house."

"Hmmm… I have no choice but to agree; cars are local," she concedes, "until they build flying cars that take us overseas."

"Yeah…" said John, gleefully, as he shuffled back to her side and they continued walking, "I can't wait for flying cars."

"Me too!" Aisha exclaimed. There was a short silence as John contemplated the future. She turned to him, requesting his eyes. "Last Christmas, while we were on holiday in California, my eldest brother, Bashir, took the rest of us to this science fair and there were so many interesting things to see. Technology that hadn't yet been released. There were these things they called 'drones' – I'm sure some Nigerians will buy it soon – they can fly really high and record videos or take pictures from the sky. It felt like a toy or video game because of the remote control you hold and use to navigate it – I had so much fun flying it.

"You flew it?!" John asked, excited.

"Yes... but only inside the dome where the science fair was holding – it was quite a high dome though – I got to take it for a test-drive. The people who made it said they'll start mass producing it by February, two thousand and ten; which was over a month ago."

"Wow... I'll check them out online," he said, as they got to the front gate of Professor Amaechi's staff quarters. "We're here."

"Is your uncle around?" Aisha asked, as she spotted the university official car parked in the compound.

"Yeah, he is but he doesn't bite."

She giggled. "I'm sure he doesn't but he's a Professor and I'm a student waltzing into his house."

John laughed. "L.O.L. He's not going to report you to your H.O.D, if that's what you're thinking." He holds open the pedestrian gate to the compound and stands aside for her to walk in.

"It crossed my mind but if you promise to stand up for me, I'll feel better," she chimed, as she entered the compound.

"Okay then. I promise." He entered too and shut the gate. He then held her right palm with his left and led her into the house. Aisha had begun to look forward to Thursdays, when she got over two hours to spend with John, before Kabiru came to pick her up. She hardly ever stayed on campus past six-thirty p.m., except when she was preparing for exams and had the excuse to stay back and 'read more'. Most days she would just hang out with her friends; Amina, Funke and Ijeoma, but Thursdays had become reserved for John. It was becoming obvious to her that she was getting attached to him; the way she would always think about him when she was alone; the way she would feel whenever she received a text message from him.

Professor Amaechi was just heading towards the staircase as they stepped into living room of the house. He had seen John walking into the compound with a young lady and he automatically decided he should give them some breathing space. This might be the first girl John was bringing over, since he moved into his house, six years ago, before the start of his university education. John was never the brawling type; he always kept his focus but it was nice to see that he had not totally missed out on his social education. He was a little curious about the purple Hijab on the pretty girl; obviously, she was a Muslim; what a strange coalition with a boy from a Catholic family.

"Good evening, Uncle," John announced. Professor Amaechi turned toward them both, acting unaware.

"Hello John."

"Good evening, sir," Aisha greeted

"Good evening," he replied, taking a better look at the girl John brought in.

"This is my friend, Aisha Mustapha." John interjected.

"Oh, that's fine," he said, taking a lingering step towards the staircase. "Are you in the same department?" The Professor asked, swinging a look at her.

"No, sir. I'm in two hundred level, Business Admin."

"Oh, I see. You're just friends then – John, don't keep her standing; get her a drink. I'm going to take a short nap upstairs. You guys have fun." He began to ascend the stairs.

"Okay, Uncle."

"Thank you, sir," Aisha beamed.

"You're welcome anytime, dear," he replied, leaving them alone downstairs. John turned to her.

"Please have a seat, your highness," he chanted to her, comically. She scoffed.

She headed towards the sofa and dropped her bag on it. "I don't really feel like sitting... but I wouldn't mind a drink – where's your kitchen?"

"Okay – follow me." He dropped his sling bag on the dining table and headed into the kitchen. Aisha followed him in, taking in a good view of the entire house; it was certainly lacking a woman's touch. It was neat but bereft of color and artistry. They entered the kitchen and John went over to open the fridge.

"How come your uncle never got married? – hope he can't hear us," she whispered, looking into the fridge as John was doing.

"He's gone into his room already – he was a Priest before but then he suddenly decided to leave the Priesthood and focus on education, but it seems he kept his vow of celibacy or just never got into a relationship with any woman." John offered her a can of cola soda. She collected it. He then took one for himself. They opened the drinks and both took sips.

"What made him leave the Priesthood?" she asked.

"He… it's a bit complicated… I think his philosophy studies, kind of, made him lose his faith – he said he didn't believe anymore that anyone needed the church; that everyone should find God within themselves and that we should each do it privately, not in groups… he said the church and other religious institutions had become 'political beasts' – in his words."

"Wow… that's a radical view of things," she let out, taking another sip of her soda. There was a short silence. Aisha was leaning on the kitchen cabinet, while John was leaning on the fridge, about two steps away from her. Suddenly, there was a bit of a tension in the room, as they realized that they were both alone, together, in a private place. John felt the tension too and came up with a distraction.

He dropped his can, pulled out his phone and opened his messaging app. He then went to lean on the cabinet beside her, opened her profile and showed it to her. "What does this mean? Ur status…"

She smiled. "…nothing."

"Really? 'Another Thursday with my bestie.' Am I your 'bestie'?" he asked, looking at her and smiling happily. She looked back at him, trying to hide her smile, and their eyes met. She wanted to answer his question but it was as though they started a new conversation with their eyes. The way he looked at her was always so perfect. He made her feel warm with his gentle eyes; he looked at her with such loyalty and dedication; he made her feel like he would always be by her side, no questions asked.

No one needed to force it; it just came naturally for her. Aisha turned to face him and leaned her lips forward towards his.

John stopped breathing as she approached him; it seemed his heart also stopped for five seconds. Their lips touched and he felt shudders, all over his body.

She shut her eyes, and she could feel thousands of electric sparkles, spiraling through her bloodstream, as she fell into him.

*****

Father John has no idea what to say until Aisha speaks. Finally, she does.

"Is it... too late?"

"Too late... for what?" John asks, struggling to understand.

"For our love story." A tear finds its way down her right eye, as she continues to hold his gaze. "These past few days have made it so obvious to me that I'm still in love with you; that I never stopped loving you, John." This is precisely what John feared; the gates to his heart being rammed open. He knew somewhere in his heart that he might fall in love with her again; he knows no woman on the planet could do this to him at this point, except her.

"Aisha... it took me four years... devotion and prayer, meditation and observing silence, to get where I am now; to get over you and move on," John protests, as a tear drops from his right eye also. "I gave you my heart and my soul – you know I did – but you turned it away... nothing could have kept me away from you, except you... you knew that and you did just enough to break my determination; to break my heart... you left me; I never spoke to you again after that evening; you never replied even one message." He pours out emotions he has been storing for years and a stream of tears follow.

"John... I had just learned my dad was about to become Emir and I had to stay away. Kabiru threatened to tell my parents and – I... I'm sorry. I could have made it work but I was scared; I was weak," she admits, "but please, give me a second chance."

"I can't, Aisha. It's too late!"

"Please... don't say that. Please... don't sentence me to a life of sadness. You hold my heart, John... you know how deep our love was."

"You should have known that too! You ruined it! You took my love for granted... and now I have had to fill my empty heart with something new. I have had to move on... and even though I did, I still kept my promise to you."

She looks down, away from his eyes. "I understand, John... I understand." She pulls out a handkerchief from her handbag and wipes her tears. "I just felt it was necessary to come over and tell you in person, what has been going on in my heart." She picks her handbag and gets up from the chair. "I'll be leaving now." She pulls out her business card from her handbag. John pulls out tissue paper from a pack on his desk and wipes his tears. "But please keep my number... and if you ever want to see me, just call me; I'll come running." She drops the card on his table, offering him her eyes once more. "Wherever you are, whatever time of the day, call me and I'll come running, John. If you give me your love again, I'll keep it and never let go..."

John avoids her gaze and disregards her card on the table. He takes a deep breath and regains composure. "Thanks for coming."

She takes that as an unmistakable signal to say no more. She knows she has upset him but at least she poured out her heart. All she can do now is hope in love. "Bye..." Aisha breathes out. She turns and heads out of his office.

She opens the door, steps out, and shuts it gently. Father John lets out the hot gashes of pain, brewing in his heart. He picks the card she left on the table and reads it:

"Vodasat Telecoms.

Aisha Mustapha.

Head of Business development."

He wishes he could hate her but what he hates, right now, is himself, for being so vulnerable to her, even after all these years. He still loves her pretty palms; he still loves the way she loves; he still loves her. He remembers why he made that promise to her, about a month to her nineteenth birthday, and why he kept the promise. He remembers the promise she made too, which she claims she has kept.

*****

"So, basically, I'm lying in my bed with – and I just kissed – someone's fiancé? And I'm going to kiss her again?" John asked, with a tone of sarcasm. They were both laying on their sides, facing each other, in John's room, upstairs of Professor Amaechi's staff quarters. She replied his question with a sincerely guilty look.

"I know I should have told you earlier but... I... I didn't want to push you away. I've been betrothed to Hassan since I was sixteen – almost three years ago," she said, poignantly. John suddenly understood the severity of her confession. The comedy was wiped from his eyes. Aisha had told him over text last night that she had a confession she wanted to make, after he had told her all about Catholic Confession in one of their lengthy conversations. It was almost a year since their first kiss, and they had said 'I love you' to each other so many times but she decided to wait this long to tell him this?

"So, you're going to marry him?" John asked, feeling his heart being crushed. She saw the pain in his eyes and tried to take it away. She placed her palm on his cheek.

"No... I won't marry him. Not if I keep falling in love with you the way that I am."

"...prove it," he demanded.

"How?" she asked, eager to prove herself.

"In confession, which is actually called the Sacrament of Penance, after you confess your sins, the Priest assigns you a penance before you receive absolution."

"So, the penance is like a fine we pay for the sin and the absolution is the forgiveness?"

"Yes, not usually money just deeds," he clarified.

"Okay," she says, fully understanding, "so... give me my penance."

"Take off your Hijab; I want to see your hair."

"What?! No! You're not a Marham, so you can't see my hair," she declared.

"What is a Marham?"

"A Marham is a close relative, parent or a spouse; those are only people allowed to see my hair."

"Oh, so that's what it's called – well, exactly my point. I don't want to not-be a Marham anymore, so prove your love to me."

He drove a valid point, considering the nature of her confession. "Okay, I will... but you have to make me a promise to me first." She sat up on the bed.

"What promise?" John lazily sat up on the bed too.

"Anything, that will prove your love for me... and I'll make a promise too before I take off my Hijab."

"Okay... I promise... that I will marry you, if you give me the chance... and if you don't, then I won't marry anyone at all."

"Wow, John!" She leaned forward and kissed him deeply. "You're crazy." She took a deep breath and got ready to make her own promise. "I promise... that I will never, ever, love anyone as much as I love you." She then kissed him again.

"Okay, my love," he whispered, intoxicated with her. She closed her eyes and began to take off her wine-red Hijab.

*****

Father John has been unable to sleep since the 'Office of Readings' midnight prayer. He also had a torturous day, all the way after his morning meeting with Aisha. Apparently, there are a lot unresolved issues between them and the feelings he thought he had buried are now erupting on the surface.

He was unable to concentrate during the Vespers; the evening prayer, and the same thing happened during the Office of Readings. Fortunately for him, the Parish Priest; Father Aderemi conducted the Vespers and Father Richard; the assistant Parish Priest, conducted the Office of Readings. This gave John's mind a lot of time to wander but his mind chose to linger on the image of the tears streaming down Aisha's face, some hours back. It hurt him to see her hurt; it made him cry to see her cry, especially knowing that he could stop her tears.

John paces around his private quarters in the church rectory. It's almost one a.m. and he can't get her off his mind. He knows he can't continue like this if he's going perform his duties faithfully; he needs closure. He walks over to his reading table and picks up his mobile phone, along with her business card. After hours of resisting, he finally decides to call her, at one a.m. He dials her number and it rings. She picks on the ninth ring.

"...hello," comes Aisha's voice, just arising out of sleep.

"It's me, Aisha; John."

"John... you called..."

"Yes... I really need to be with you tonight."

She takes a moment to gather her racing heart. "...me too," she whispers.

CHAPTER 7

Kabiru picked up Ijeoma at her apartment in Ajah, about thirty minutes ago, for another clandestine evening of fun, with his two childhood friends; Hassan and Rasheed. He and Ijeoma have been close since his university days. He met her through his younger sister; Aisha, and they have been involved with each other, secretly, for over five years. He has made it clear to Ijeoma that they might never get married and she claims to be okay with that, as long as they can still be together, once in a while, like tonight. He drives through Victoria Island, with his stereo turned up, heading towards Hassan's high-rise apartment, where the boys are waiting.

Kabiru just got into Lagos from Kano on Tuesday afternoon; yesterday, with his mother; Karida. She had come to Lagos to prepare for her old friend's daughter's marriage. Habibat happened to be the first real friend Karida made, after moving to Nigeria with her husband; Alhaji Mustapha, in the year nineteen eighty-two.

Karida was born and raised in Saudi Arabia, being an extended member of the Saudi Arabian royal family; the House of Saud. After her own Nikah in Saudi Arabia, Karida then moved to Nigeria with her husband, Aliu Mustapha, and she was well taken care of by his family, being his fifth wife, but in those first few years in Nigeria, Habibat was the only one she could let her guard down with, apart from her husband. She was the first wife of one of Aliu's close friends.

Alhaja Habibat's daughter's Nikah is scheduled to hold this Friday and Karida came prepared to represent herself, her children and her husband; the Emir of Kano, at the joyous event. Alhaji Mustapha could not make it to Lagos for the wedding, even though he is old friends with the father of the bride, because of the great responsibilities now vested on his shoulders. Habibat, even more than her husband, was disappointed Alhaji Mustapha wouldn't be able to attend; she had hoped to wow her the guests with the presence of the Emir of Kano. As a result, Karida is putting in an effort to ensure her husband's presence is felt at the Nikah, this Friday.

Kabiru drives in through the main gate of the 1004 apartments. He then drives over to block B, where Hassan's apartment is. The Nikah, this Friday, was a great excuse to come to Lagos with Karida, in the guise of looking out for his mother. Ever since he moved to Kano with his family, he has been under close scrutiny. He has had to behave in a manner fitting for the son of the Emir of Kano. He and Danladi now live permanently in Kano, with their father and mother, working to oversee daily activities at the Gidan Rumfa; the Emir's palace. Bashir, the oldest son, remained in Abuja to continue managing

Ibro Capital; the parent company of all their father's subsidiary businesses and investments.

Once in a while, like these few days in Lagos, Kabiru gets the opportunity to leave the Gidan Rumfa and live, temporarily, like he is not the Emir's son. He parks the BMW X5 in front of Block B.

Ijeoma shoots him a look. "Do I need to take my handbag?"

"Ummm… not really, we won't spend more than thirty minutes here before heading out again," he clarifies.

"Okay… in that case, I'll just leave everything here."

Kabiru steps out of the car and Ijeoma does the same. They walk towards Block B, with the cool nighttime breeze brushing past them. She walks in front, while he follows. This is not the first time she has come to Hassan's apartment with Kabiru. She got to know Rasheed Aregbesola also, even before he got married. Those two have always been notorious womanizers; she doesn't remember seeing the same women with them, whenever they all went out together. She can't really tell if Kabiru sees other women also but he certainly not as much as them because he spends most of his time with her, whenever he's in Lagos, and in Kano he is with his fiancé.

"Ah-ah, babe, this your waist just keeps getting smaller, every time I see you," Kabiru flirts. She chuckles.

"Stop it."

"Hot-hot mama!"

"Did you miss me?" she asks, swinging her eyes back at him.

"You know I did," he replies sincerely.

"You're going to have to prove it," she says, disbelievingly. They step into Block B and head for the elevator. Hassan stays on the top floor. Ijeoma pushes the button, requesting the lift.

"...I did bring you back a gift – it's in the car; I'll give it to you later tonight.

"I don't need gifts, Kabiru." The elevator doors open and a young Indian man steps out. They both step in, alone. Ijeoma pushes the number-seven button and the elevator doors shut. She then grabs his palm and pulls him towards her as the lift ascends. "I don't need gifts," she repeats, leaning her back on the wall of the elevator, waiting for his lips to connect with hers, "just love me." He lets go of her palm and places both his hands around her waist. He leans his chest on hers and kisses her, while pulling her waist towards his. She puts her palms around his neck and kisses him back, slowly. He moves his left hand up her back and his right hand down her thighs.

The elevator comes to a halt. They slowly detach from each other as the doors open. They take one naughty look at each other and then step onto the seventh floor. Ijeoma walks behind him as they head down the balcony corridor.

"How is Aisha?" she asks.

"She's fine. We just had dinner before I left the house. Usman came over with his wife and son – when last did you talk to her?"

"You know I haven't spoken to Aisha in ages – over five years… I guess we don't have that much in common anymore."

"You have me in common and you know Hassan, who is her fiancé."

"Exactly! Both things I can't speak to her about; I doubt it would be wise to tell her that her fiancé is a womanizer or that her brother is cheating on his fiancé with me," she chimes. Kabiru laughs.

"Would you consider you-and-me as cheating?" he asks, looking into her eyes, as they get to Hassan's front door. She returns the same loving look.

"No, I won't call it cheating... but your fiancé certainly will," she says before giving him a peck on the lips. He giggles and then knocks on the door. Hassan comes over to open the door.

"My man!" Hassan exclaims, as he sees Kabiru.

"Brother!" They shake hands firmly, smiling at each other.

"Hi Hassan," Ijeoma says.

"Ijeoma, nice to see you again." They enter the apartment and Hassan shuts the door. Kabiru and Ijeoma walk towards the living room, with Hassan walking behind them, and see Rasheed sitting with two young ladies.

"I heard the bad-man is in town!" Rasheed howls, as he gets up and heads towards Kabiru.

"You heard correctly!" Kabiru exclaims. He shakes Rasheed firmly.

"You left us in Lagos with all the booze and beautiful ladies, and went to live like an Imam in Kano, right?"

"Why are you complaining? Me gone means there's more for you!" The three men laugh.

"Meet my new friends; Funmi and Sandra," Rasheed announces, gesturing towards the two young ladies. The girls smile back in response. Ijeoma goes ahead to take a seat, while they continue with their pleasantries, feeling a little ignored. "This is the Emir of Kano's son; he's a bad-man bad-boy!" Rasheed sings to the two girls. They giggle in response.

"Why are you spoiling my name? I am a changed man now; I drive slow now."

"You? You, changed man? ...meanwhile, we have something important to talk about," Rasheed ends with a serious look.

"So important that you can't even say hello to my babe?"

"Ah... Ijeoma, I'm sorry o!" Rasheed offers her a guilty look. "You know you are like one of the guys."

"It's okay; don't mind Kabiru," Ijeoma says, smiling.

"What do you want to talk to me about?" Kabiru asks.

"Should we talk now?"

"Yeah, why not?

"Okay, lets step outside," Rasheed says, heading away from the living room and towards the front door.

"Sure." Kabiru follows.

"So, I'm not invited to this gist?" Hassan asks Rasheed.

"It's for the big boys only."

"Fool!" Hassan spurts. Rasheed ignores him and opens the front door.

The two men step out through the front door, and onto the balcony corridor, overlooking the estate from the top floor. Rasheed pulls out his pack of cigarettes and offers it to Kabiru. He collects one and then Rasheed takes one for himself also. Rasheed lights his cigarette and passes the lighter over to Kabiru, who also lights his.

"So... what is it?" Kabiru asks, curious.

"It's a serious matter o... Aisha is seeing someone else."

"My sister?"

"Yes," Rasheed says, sternly, "yesterday morning, around six a.m., I saw her leaving the Oriental Hotel, with a guy."

"You shouldn't jump into conclusions, Rasheed."

"Look, I am not stupid; I know when a man and a woman are being intimate – not to mention, this was six a.m. in the morning, and not in the evening. I checked with the hotel management and I learnt that she booked the room late that night and the guy was there with her, through the night. My father owns fifty percent of that hotel, so I have full access to the management."

"This is not good," Kabiru says, looking away from Rasheed.

"I have been trying to act cheerful since I got here, so I don't end up telling Hassan, but you know I can't keep quiet for long. Hassan and I go way back; he won't forgive me if I kept this from him. I have kept this information for more than twenty-four hours now and that's long enough. I have to tell him tonight."

"Wait, Rasheed. Apply caution. Tell me exactly all you know..."

*****

"Our Classic Deluxe is one hundred thousand Naira, per stay," the female receptionist said.

"Okay, I'll take that, please," Aisha confirmed, pulling out her ATM card from her handbag.

"Okay, madam." She collected the card from Aisha and continued pushing some buttons on her screen.

"Your name, please?"

"Aisha... Mustapha," Aisha said, hesitantly.

She then stuck the card into the point-of-sale machine. Aisha entered her card pin and waited a little longer.

Her heart was pure; she knew that it was love that had led her here and not lust, or vanity. She knew she must take the necessary steps, if the night went as she thought it would, to make her dream a reality; to sever her relationship with Hassan and give herself fully to John.

The receptionist handed back her card and also a card-key for room six-o-nine. "Have a wonderful stay, madam."

"I... am expecting someone."

"Okay, I will call your room phone as soon as anyone comes by."

"Thanks. I'll also pass on the room number to... the person," Aisha said before heading towards the elevator, clutching her handbag. The meticulously polished hotel lobby was quiet and mostly empty, as it should be at one forty-five a.m. Aisha had thrown on her purple Abaya and purple Hijab to come here. She asked Nuru to drive her here, all the way thinking about the life-changes to come. Her mother had called her about five hours ago, to tell her that she would be arriving in Lagos today; Tuesday.

Aisha pushed the button, requesting the elevator. It opened immediately. She stepped into the empty elevator and pushed the number-six button. The doors shut and the lift ascended. Karida had promised her, on her nineteenth birthday, that she would support her if she ever decided she didn't want to marry Hassan, and so

Aisha was planning to tell her mother exactly that, if this night went as she thought it would.

Aisha's phone rang. She pulled it out of her handbag. It was John calling. She picked up the call as the elevator doors opened, to the sixth floor.

"Hello."

"Hi... I am just outside the Oriental Hotel now. What room are you in?

"Room six-o-nine," she replied, walking down the hallway.

"Okay, I'll be there shortly."

"Okay." She put down her phone. She got to room six-o-nine and inserted the card-key, before opening the door. She was feeling anxious, tense and a little scared, at the same time. She shut the door and went over to drop her handbag on the table. The view of the ambient room did help a little, to calm her nerves. She opened the fridge, just beside the table, and pulled out a cola soda. She opened it and took a sip, before taking a deep breath. This meant a lot to her; her heart was hanging in the balance here; John was everything to her now; he was the love of her life.

The hotel-room phone rang. Aisha walked over to the side of the bed to pick it up.

"Hello."

"Hello, Madam. Mr. John is here to see you," the receptionist informed her, over the phone.

"Yes, please let him up."

"Alright, madam." Aisha put down the phone and sat on the side of the bed. This was the first time in over four years that she would be alone with John, in a private place. Ever since they reunited, just some days back, there had been this wall between them, one that never used to be there. She did everything she could, to bring down that wall and she hoped she had succeeded. This night was going to tell.

She walked over to the mirror, to stare at her face. It's amazing how she thought she could just walk away from John and never look back. It's amazing how she could live without him for four years. He would cross her mind now and then but she would justify staying away from him because he wasn't Muslim; or because she had to choose between her father and him; but mostly because, as the years passed, she thought he could never forgive her. That all changed when she looked into his gentle, loving eyes again.

She heard a knock on the door and hurriedly went over to open it. She saw John, dressed in a black button-up shirt, black pants and black shoes, and smiled at him. He looked back at her but didn't smile in return; he just kept on a tense look. Aisha stepped aside for him to enter and shut the door behind him. He stood close the entrance, not yet willing to go in. She decided to lead the way. She walked past him and into the room. He suddenly grabbed her palm as she passed in front of him and pulled her back, towards himself. He wrapped his hands around her waist and kissed her passionately. Aisha's heart throbbed violently and she found herself out of breath. It was as though she was drowning but the only difference was that she was not struggling; she wanted to drown, under his kiss.

*****

The family dinner had ended about two hours ago. Usman came over to the family house with his wife; Zynat and his one-year old son; Hameed. They just left about thirty minutes ago, for their home in Victoria Island, and her mother went upstairs to retire for the day. Karida is not as young as she used to be but she is still as beautiful; Aisha knows where she got her beauty from. Kabiru also got dressed and left, about an hour ago. He took one of the cars in the compound and he is most likely going to be back tomorrow morning.

Aisha walks out of her room and steps onto the corridor, leading to her mother's room. She had hoped to have some private time with her mother tonight, seeing as everything went so well with John last night. All through the dinner, she kept feeling like she was carrying a big secret and she wants to unburden herself of it. The first and most important person to confide in is her mother. She knocks on Karida's door.

"Come in," Karida announces. Aisha enters and sees her mother lying on the bed.

"I need to talk to you, mommy."

"Okay, dear. What about?" Karida asks, sensing the seriousness in Aisha's tone. She walks over and sits at the foot of her mother's bed.

"It's about me... and my future... mom, I don't want to marry Hassan anymore."

"Na-Uzo-Billah," Karida exclaims, displeased, before sitting up on the bed. "Why, Aisha?"

"I can't spend the rest of my life with him... and... I'm in love with someone else."

"You must guard your heart, my daughter. You can't allow yourself to fall in love unnecessarily. Our family is in a political position now and as such we need to keep powerful friends and allies. General Ibrahim has gone extra lengths for your father and his son has been waiting for you, for over ten years, and now you change your mind?"

"This was never my decision; I never chose Hassan," Aisha protests, "and you promised me, on my nineteenth birthday, that you would stand by me if I ever decided I didn't want to marry him."

"Oh, so now you're going to use my words against me? Very wise of you," Karida grunts.

"Help me, mother," Aisha says, trying to convince her mother of her honest intentions.

"My daughter, you know I would do anything for you but not everything is within my power... I will talk to your father when I get back to the Gidan Rumfa but I am quite sure he would object to this. Still, like I promised, I will stand by you. It might take a while for your father to get used to the idea and eventually agree, and you have to be willing to do your best to convince him."

"Thank you - thank you!" Aisha exclaims, beaming happily.

"Don't thank me yet... and who is this your new 'love'? I hope he's from a respectable Muslim family... is he?"

Aisha hesitates to answer.

*****

It was over thirty minutes past three a.m. and Father John should have been observing the Morning Lauds, with the rest of the Clergy but instead, he was laying on a bed beside Aisha, at the Oriental Hotel. They were both laying on their sides, facing each other, fully dressed except for their shoes, with his right fingers locked into her left fingers.

"You just became a Priest three months ago?"

"Yeah... after four years in the Seminary and more as a deacon - that's basically where I spent the last seven years." He then changed the topic; "how about you; where did you spend the last almost-seven years?"

"Well, I graduated five years ago and went to do my Youth Service Orientation. During that period, I started working at Vodasat telecoms – finished my Orientation and started working full-time at Vodasat for a year, before going to get two masters degrees – spent two years in the UK... came back and got a better job at Vodasat."

"How about your fiancé? Are you still betrothed to him?" He asked the impending question.

"...yes... but I'm ready to leave him, if you tell me I should." John looked away from her. He never knew fate would deal him these cards but now he had to make the difficult decision, to be with her or not. He kept quiet and so did Aisha, for a while. She then moved her body even closer to his.

"Do you want to make love to me?" she asked, softly. John couldn't find the words to say in response. He took a few deep breaths. "I'm still a virgin but... I always wanted it to be you... if you want to, I'll give myself to you. I kept my promise; I never, ever loved anyone as much as I love you," she concluded.

John leaned his head forward and kissed her deeply. "Let's wait, my love. We both have to take certain

steps before we can be together, without feeling guilty…
for now I am satisfied with your body close to mine."

CHAPTER 8

"I know we are a political family, mommy," Aisha says quickly, trying to make some sense before her mother shuts down the conversation, "and I have put that into consideration –

"No, you have not. If you had, you won't be considering this. Your father will never agree to such! Do you know how many ways his antagonists can use this against him?" Karida asks, scolding.

"The love between John and I could be a sign of peace! Daddy has always spoken about a future where Christians and Muslims would live together freely, with no limitations, even before he became Emir – you say the same thing too, mother. This could be an opportunity for us to be the political family that preaches peace... and unity," Aisha finally gets her point in. Her mother looks away, finding it hard to refute her daughter. Aisha continues, desperately hanging on this last string of hope, "John is a loving person and he is giving up a lot too; he is going to be under great scrutiny from his people but he is willing to endure all that because he loves me... and I love him; with every part of me, I love him. His heart is pure," Aisha concludes, allowing tears to stream down her face freely, in the presence of her mother, hoping that Karida would see how deep this love is. Karida looks back into Aisha's watery eyes.

"This love between you and... this John, could also be a sign of war. Peace is not so easy to come by. We have to tread carefully," Karida explicates softly.

She signals for Aisha to come closer, by patting the surface of the bed beside her. Aisha then climbs onto the bed and goes to sit, with her back perched up, beside her mother. She lays her head gently on her Karida's shoulder. Her mother then swings her left arm around her and pets her gently, trying to assuage her tears.

"Thank you," Aisha whispers.

"If you say this John is worth fighting for, then I'll certainly be fighting on your side... so, tell me more about him," Karida urges, eager to know more about her daughter's heartthrob.

*****

Rasheed Aregbesola drove down Ozumbe Mbadiwe street, at four-thirty a.m., eager to puts his hands all over the young, prepossessing girl that was seated beside him. He had met her at the Ikoyi branch of Golden Bank; one of his father's companies. He stepped in to make a quick transaction on a Monday morning and was escorted upstairs to a private meeting room. Soon, someone had come to attend to him and he was surprised to see the new face. Rasheed knew almost all the staff at the Ikoyi branch of Golden Bank, certainly the pretty ones, because it was the most convenient and closest branch to his house at Banana Island, and all the staff at the branch certainly knew who he was; the son of their employer. He bore a striking resemblance to his father; Chief Aregbesola, and if that wasn't enough, the Manager at the Ikoyi branch had certainly made it clear by going extra lengths to please Rasheed whenever he stepped in. He had certainly put on a show for Rasheed by getting the pretty recruit to handle his transaction. He found out that her name was Funmi; she had started working for the bank about a month ago, just after her Youth Service Orientation.

Rasheed had employed charm and imposed power, just to get her to have dinner with him that evening, after work. He then utilized deception and distracted with humor, all so he could make her stay out late with him on a Monday night. Finally, he impressed and outdid himself by convincing her to share a room with him at the Oriental Hotel, after late drinks at one of the private lounges he is fond of. He had broken down all her defenses and soon he could do all the licentious things he had been imagining doing to her, since he laid eyes on her, less than twenty-four hours ago.

He drove in through the gates of the Oriental Hotel and then went over to park the black Mercedes M Class. He stepped out and so did Funmi, holding her handbag. They headed towards the hotel reception.

"What am I going to wear to work, now?" she whined, still in the euphoria of being desired by Chief Aregbesola's son.

"Come on, that is no problem at all. I'll personally help you take off your clothes and take them to the hotel drycleaner, who's going to return them clean and ironed in about an hour, and then you can pick up a new top or blazer at the mall in the morning, if you feel like."

"You're not taking off my clothes," Funmi asserted.

Rasheed chuckled. "So, how are we going to dry-clean them?"

"He'll have to dry-clean them while I'm still in them." They stepped into the hotel lobby, passing through the automatic sliding doors.

"I am only trying to help," he said, leaning his body close to hers, as they headed towards the reception.

"Help indeed," she jibed, nudging him away with her shoulder. They got to the lady at the reception. She recognized Rasheed Aregbesola immediately, as this was not her first time attending to him.

"Good morning, sir!" the lady saluted, eager for a tip.

"Morning. Can I have the Junior Suite?"

"Yes, sir; that's a hundred and seventy thousand Naira. Do I charge it to your account?"

"Yes."

*****

It was five forty-five a.m. and Father John knew he had to return to the parish, in time for the six-thirty a.m. Mass. He put on his shoes, sitting on the side of the bed. Aisha was also getting ready to leave the hotel. She was missing the Fajr prayer this morning, having spent the whole night awake. She stood up from her side of the bed, having put on her shoes and went over to pick up her handbag laying on the table. She pulled out her phone.

"You came here with a taxi, right?" she asked.

"Yes, I did," he said, standing up also.

"Let me request a taxi for you with my phone."

"Thanks."

Aisha wanted to leave the Hotel early also, to avoid any unwanted encounters. She picked her bag and headed outside the room, while requesting a Taxi on her phone. John walked closely behind her. He leaned over her shoulder and opened the door for her, seeing as both her hands were occupied.

"Thanks," she said, looking back at him. They stepped out onto the hallway and he shut the door; it locked automatically.

"Are you with the key?" he asked.

"Yes, it's in my bag." They headed towards the elevator. "I just got you a taxi; it's almost downstairs –

sorry, I'll put my phone away soon; I just need to call my driver." She pushed the screen and then put the phone to her ear.

"It's okay," he said, walking slowly beside her.

"Nuru," Aisha said into the Phone, "please come to the lobby with the car." She then put her phone down and dipped it into her bag, breathing a sigh of relief. "I wish we could just stay here and never go back." She put her free palm in his.

"The same thing I was thinking... sometime soon, we will," John said as they got to the elevator. He pushed the request button and it lit up, as they waited for the lift.

"My mom is coming back today and I'm going to tell her about us, hopefully tomorrow evening, after she's settled in." John listened to her, feeling a little tense about the decisions he also had to make.

"I am supposed to handle the Mass this morning, at the Parish, but I have to recuse myself; I can't say Mass anymore," he said, looking at the floor, "what I am going to do is make a confession to the Parish Priest about the intentions of my heart and then write a letter to the Pope, at the Vatican City, asking for permission to leave the Priesthood – he would probably decline but at least I would have followed due process. I'll also have to see the

Archbishop; Most Reverend Alexander, to let him know that I'll be leaving the Archdiocese and explain in detail, why," John talked on, until the elevator doors opened. They both stepped into the empty elevator.

"I know I am asking you for a lot, John." Aisha felt guilty. John pushed the elevator button, for the ground floor.

"I want it too… I just wish you didn't have to wait seven years to come to your senses," John spurted. Aisha giggled as the elevator doors closed.

"I was crazy enough to think that I'll forget about you. I'm sorry." She embraced him and leaned her head on his chest. He embraced her too and they held on. "I don't want to spend another moment away from you. We need to find time again."

"We will, my love. I'll sneak out again, in a few days," he ended, a little comically. She tittered, rising slightly above the heavy feeling of loneliness looming around her. The last time she felt this good was over seven years ago but it was short-lived and she had to be apart from him again. She continued to hold on to him, relishing the last few moments of being alone together. The elevator then came to a halt at the ground floor. They slowly detached as the doors slid open.

*****

Rasheed woke up in the chilly, dark room and reached for his phone beside the bed. He tapped the screen and his alcohol-blurred vision was hurt by the bright light. He checked the time and it was five-thirty a.m. A knock on the door had woken him up. He checked and saw Funmi beside him, still deep in sleep.

He heard the knock on the door again. He got out from under the bed quilt, wearing only his boxers. He walked over to the door and opened it. There was a bell attendant, standing at the entrance, holding Funmi's dry-cleaned clothes.

"Good morning, sir," the bell attendant said.

"Thank you. Let me have them." Rasheed collected the hanger from him and hurriedly shut the door. He preferred to leave the room before she woke up. The last thing he wanted was to have to indulge unnecessary pillow-talk. He had fun with her and he was proud of the fact that he got what he wanted but now he had to return home, to his wife. He hung her clothes on the wardrobe knob, where she would be able to see them, when she woke up. He then went over to the side of his bed, quietly, and hurriedly put on his clothes, which were spread across the floor.

After getting dressed, he went over to the table and pulled out a small sheet of paper and a pen; part of the hotel stationery. He scribbled quickly:

'You look better with your
clothes off.

Lol. Call me.'

He pulled out his business card from his pocket and placed it beside the note. He then headed outside the room, while Funmi slept on. He stepped onto the hallway and shut the door quietly.

He headed towards the elevator. He couldn't even ease himself in the bathroom, to avoid waking her up, so now he was going to have to use the men's room in the hotel lobby.

*****

Rasheed stepped out of the men's room at the far end of the hotel lobby, feeling relieved, but still under the hangover, from a long night. He decided to have a cup of coffee and some cake to spring himself back to life. He walked across the lobby and into the glass-walled café, just in front of the elevator.

"Good morning, sir," said the male café attendant. It was about ten minutes to six a.m.; Rasheed saw from the wall clock.

"Morning. Can I have a Café Latte please," Rasheed said. He then pointed to the vanilla cake in the show glass; "and some of that cake."

"Yes, sir," he said. It was then that the elevator doors slid open and Rasheed saw Aisha Mustapha just letting go of a gentleman she was tightly embracing. He was thunderstruck; he even doubted what he saw. They didn't notice anyone staring at them through the glass wall, obscured by the confectionary shelves. He saw them step out of the lift and then they walked closely beside each other, heading towards the reception, and then out of his view. He had to be a hundred-percent sure of what he was seeing; soon enough he found himself walking out of the café.

"Sir! Your order?" the attendant asked, confused.

"I'm coming," he said and continued out. He stopped out of view, behind one of the giant pillars. Aisha just finished dropping off the hotel key with the receptionist, with the man standing beside her. They then headed outside the lobby together. Her black Mercedes S class was waiting at the entrance. She turned around and gave him another tight embrace before stepping into her car; Rasheed knew her car quite well. She was driven off and then a blue Toyota Corolla stopped to pick up the guy.

He went straight for the hotel lobby. "Do you know those people that just left?" he asked the receptionist. She hesitated but then remembered that his father; Chief Aregbesola, was a part owner of the hotel.

"Errm… Miss Aisha Mustapha, sir," she said, foregoing protocol.

"What was she doing here? When did she check in?" he badgered on.

"She… checked in last night, sir, around two a.m."

"What about the man, was he with her?

"He came some minutes after she got here."

"What is his name?"

"Errmm…" she hummed, looking at her records, "Mr. John."

"John who?" he asked incredulously.

*****

"Babe… babe, wake up… you need to drop me at my apartment," Ijeoma nags, tapping Kabiru lightly. He wakes up lazily, after their wild night, touring three clubs on the Lagos island, with Hassan, Rasheed, Funmi and her friend; Sandra. Kabiru had too much to drink and he is finding it hard to remember exactly where he is at the moment.

"Are we in Hassan's house?

"Yes."

"How did we…?"

"I had to drive us back from the club; you had a little too much fun for your age." She pecks him on the cheek. He finally takes full control of his body and sits up.

"So, you drove me home?" he asks, feeling slightly embarrassed, "you must have been laughing at me." She laughed, covering her mouth with her hand.

"It's okay, baby," she says convincingly, "you can rely on me to take care of you, anytime."

"So, that means that we didn't end the night the expected way.

"Nope... you slept off, so I slept off too."

"And you want to leave this morning?" he asks, dissatisfied.

"I have a job, oga. We can pick up where we left off later."

"I have told you repeatedly, to quit working at that place. Let me get you a job at Vodasat or another big company."

"And I have also told you, repeatedly, that I like my job and I don't want to work for your family, under your watchful eyes," she retorts, "I want to be free; just love me."

"I disagree. This is no longer a negotiation. You officially quit your job today because…" Kabiru stands up from the bed, shoving away the effects of the hangover, and heads towards the open door, wearing his inner vest and boxers, "I am not dropping you at your apartment this morning…" He continues towards the door. He then quickly steps out of the room, knowing that the key is on the other side, shuts the door and locks her inside. "And I'm not letting you leave either. Tell your Boss you have been kidnapped!"

Ijeoma rushes towards the door, just realizing what he was planning. "Kabiru, noo! Stop it! I neeed to get to work today."

"What is inside the work that you're running to? Are you sure you're not in love with your boss?"

"And what if I am? It's none of your business! You don't own me!"

"You are taken; let him know."

"There's no room for me in your life, Kabiru. So, let me go," she pleads.

"You can be mine, Ijeoma; even if we don't get married," he says gently, through the locked door.

"Stop it, Kabiru… just go back to your fiancé and let me go to my work."

"Well, not today. You have been kidnapped." He leaves her and heads down the steps of Hassan's 1004 apartment.

Ijeoma continues to bang on the door. "Kabiru! Kabiru!!" He ignores her, looking for his two friends, wanting to have a more detailed recap of last night.

He perceives the scent of tobacco coming from the small balcony behind the parlor. He gets downstairs, walks over and opens the glass door. He sees Rasheed and Hassan, smoking cigarettes, leaning on the balcony together.

"What's up my men?!" he exclaims, trying to rediscover his euphoria. For some reason, the other two don't respond at all but he hardly seems to notice. "Give me a cigarette, man!" he says, to Rasheed. He obliges him and offers him the pack.

"Kabiru…" Hassan starts, looking away from him, "Rasheed has told me that he saw Aisha with an unknown guy – he has told you already." Kabiru looks at Rasheed, betrayed. He had warned him not speak yet. Rasheed looks away from him. "This puts your family honor in jeopardy; I hope you know."

"Relax, Hassan. Let us handle this like men. I have known Aisha all my life and I can vouch for her honor. If there is something going on, then we need to investigate it carefully before taking any decision."

"Who is the guy?" Hassan asks him.

"I don't know –"

"His name is 'John' – sorry, I forgot to mention that last night," Rasheed adds.

"John?" Kabiru asks, irritated, "that same guy?"

"What same guy?" Hassan asks.

"There was this once – the only time Aisha misbehaved a little, when she was in university – it was with a John guy," Kabiru divulges, "we need to find out if it's the same person. In the meantime, let's keep this between us. If we find this John guy, we will handle him the way men handle men."

"Forget that! If I catch him, he's a dead man. Nobody will find his body; trust me," Hassan spews, before taking the last drag of his cigarette. The other two men look at him, unsure of what to say.

CHAPTER 9

Nuru drives his Madam; Aisha Mustapha, in the black Mercedes S class, along Adeola Odeku street, in Victoria Island, Lagos. Abu; the substitute driver and second bodyguard, sits in the front passenger seat. It's a Thursday morning and Aisha is on her way to her office at Vodasat Telecoms, hoping the day would go smoothly, and worried about what the next couple of days would bring.

She had unburdened her heart to her mother and, at first, it felt like a heavy load of worries was lifted off her but soon after, the reality of things dawned on her and now she is worried, again. Now her mother had requested to meet John and soon after she would tell the news to her father, who would want to meet John also, and so would her brothers. Her idea was gradually developing into a plan and the toughest part of this plan remained the fact that she was a Muslim woman.

According to popular Islamic belief, it is Haram for a Muslim woman to marry a non-Muslim man, even though it is permissible for a Muslim man to marry a Jewish or Christian woman. This is because it is believed that the husband ends up possessing his wife, physically, mentally and spiritually, and not the other way around. As a result, the ideals of the husband are what will be passed on to the wife and inevitably, the children. This means that if her father and brothers agree to her plans, she will still be expected to persuade John to convert to Islam.

Her decision not to marry Hassan happens to be less complicated because, according to Islamic beliefs, she has the right to consent to him as her husband or not. Even though it is wiser not to blatantly disregard her father's wishes, which is why she is after breaking the news to her father, gently, with the help of her mother.

Still, letting them know she doesn't want to marry Hassan is less than half of the plan. Now she must also tell them she wants to marry John but she cannot see herself doing the final part; telling John to leave the way of life he has been used to, so that they could get married. According to her studies, Aisha had never seen a place in the Qur'an, where it expressly said that she could not marry a Christian man but it was the common belief, and how could she argue with the whole Muslim community?

Aisha's phone rings, interrupting her heavy thoughts. She dips her hand into her handbag to pull it out, just as Nuru drives into the Vodasat Telecoms compound. She doesn't recognize the number but she goes ahead to pick the call.

"Hello..." Aisha says.

"Hiiii Aisha!" a female voice blares, seemingly excited.

"Hi… who's this?"

"Guess."

"I… have no idea…" Aisha sings, oblivious.

"Your best friend from back in the day; Ijeoma."

"Ijeoma from University?" she asks, flabbergasted.

"Yeah."

"Wow! You remembered me todayyy?"

"Oh please, you're the one that me forget me; you disappeared to London after youth service and the next thing we heard is that you've become a boss at Vodasat."

"Oh please, which boss? Nice to hear from you, dear." Nuru parks just adjacent to the entrance but Aisha remains inside the car, still engulfed in her conversation.

"Yes o, it's nice to hear you too. I ran into your brother, emmm – what's his name… Kabiru – he gave me your number."

"Yeah, he got into town on Tuesday. Wow... your voice brings back so many memories!"

Ijeoma laughs. "All our University days – I miss you too. What are you doing tomorrow? Let's hang out and catch up."

"Tomorrow... I have a wedding to attend – you should come. I'll send you an invite – where do you work now?"

"I work at Retro Media; it's a media agency on the island."

Aisha finally steps out of the car, so does Abu. He escorts her towards the entrance of the Vodasat head office, while she talks on the phone. "I will get my driver to bring you an invite to the Nikah tomorrow, this afternoon..."

*****

"Okay, I'll be expecting it... see you tomorrow then... bye." Ijeoma puts down her phone, sneering at

Kabiru seated beside her, even more unhappy with what he was making her do. Rasheed and Hassan had been sitting across her, in the living room of Hassan's house, staring at her intensely; coercing her to go along with their plans.

"So?" Kabiru asks, uttering the minds of the other two men.

"She… invited me to a wedding tomorrow."

"Cool… I'm going to be at the Nikah tomorrow also."

"So, I have to pretend that I don't know you?" she queries Kabiru, scrupulously, "…so much pretense; it's really not my style. I don't like this plan at all. What will Aisha think of me when she finds out? It's bad enough I haven't spoken to her in ages and now the first time I call her, it's to lie and spy on her."

"Look, Ijeoma. You are one of us now," Rasheed cuts in, "firstly, Aisha is never going to find out. Secondly, this information you're helping us collect is going to serve the purpose of protecting Aisha and her family's honor. You knew this John guy in University and you knew when he and Aisha were… having whatever they were having. So, you're the best person to talk to her about him. All we want to find out is what this John guy does now; where he works or where he stays and that's it. We will handle the rest."

"What do you mean by handle the rest? I hope you're not planning to do something violent. Aisha has always been smart and now she is a woman. You should leave her to make her own decisions or –"

"It's not that simple, Ijeoma. She's a Muslim woman," Kabiru interrupts.

"So, what? Because she's a Muslim woman, it means she doesn't have human rights?" she barks at him.

"Let us…" Kabiru says, changing the topic and grabbing her palm tenderly, "go and get breakfast. Leave these two old men – we'll talk about this privately."

Ijeoma decides to let go of the brewing argument. She stands up, picks her handbag and heads towards the front door, without even bothering to say goodbye to Rasheed or Hassan. Kabiru smiles at both guys, consoling them for her volatile reaction.

"I'll see you guys later," Kabiru says, standing up also, ready to leave.

"I'm leaving also. I have to go home to Binta and then stop by at the office briefly." Rasheed stands up and shakes hands with Hassan briefly. He and Kabiru then head outside the house.

There is a certain silence as they leave. Neither Kabiru nor Rasheed want to speak too much on the subject but it is becoming obvious that Hassan's ego has been deeply bruised and as a result, he might take this all too far. They both step out the front door and shut it.

Hassan has been harboring private plans of his own, while his two friends have been concocting solutions. He knows he wants to handle this scandal privately, even though the discovery was made by Rasheed, and unfortunately Kabiru had also gotten a hold of the information, who also passed it to Ijeoma. As soon as Rasheed had told him the shameful news, he already knew how to confirm it and most importantly, how to discover who this 'John' is, and where to find him. He just didn't want to have to involve Rasheed, and especially not Kabiru, who is Aisha's brother. No matter what, Kabiru would take his sister's side first and Hassan is not interested in protecting any side; all he wants is to see justice done, his own way.

If Aisha is guilty then she will pay and if this 'John' is guilty too, he will pay a thousand times. Hassan picks up his phone and dials a contact; he calls the one person who can tell him all he wants to know.

*****

Things had not gone as he had planned but in a way, they had gone as he had hoped. When deciding to join the Catholic monastery after his university education, Father John did not think that he would be seeking permission to leave the Priesthood, just three months after becoming a Priest, but he knows that he had first devoted his heart to Aisha before devoting it to the Clergy, and even though the former had crushed his heart and left him alone, he had hoped that one day he would rediscover that love. His hopes had now been made a reality but not without a price.

The Uber taxi drives him down Awolowo road, Ikoyi, and towards the Cathedral of the Holy Cross; the Roman Catholic Archdiocese of Lagos. It's a Friday morning and he has an eleven-a.m. appointment with Archbishop Alexander Williams; the Metropolitan of Lagos.

Father John meditates about the honesty of his intentions, in preparation for his meeting with the Archbishop. After his confession to his Parish Priest; Father Aderemi Etomi, he was advised to take the proper steps towards his voluntary Laicization; which involved getting the permission of the Archbishop and most importantly, that of the Pope.

It is common news that Pope Francis had recently been opening discussions about married Priests, in a bid to address the growing shortage of Catholic Priests across the world. There have been talks about reinstating Priests who had abandoned the Clergy for reasons of love or marriage. However, John's case was quite peculiar because he was in love with a Muslim woman and this is something the Roman Catholic Church generally cautioned against. So, John had decided the best thing to do was to seek a dispensation from the Priesthood and from his obligation of celibacy, which could only be granted by the Pope. He had already written a letter to the Pope yesterday, which he sent by express delivery, and now he wanted to get the approval, and consequent recommendation, of the Metropolitan of his Archdiocese, for what is called a voluntary Laicization; a request to be released from all clerical responsibilities.

The taxi driver circles around the Onikan roundabout and then on towards the Catholic mission road, where the Holy Cross Cathedral is. Father John can feel a bitter liquid running over his tongue and down his throat, like he drank a jar of ink; this feeling is the realization of his hypocrisy. Some weeks ago, he was amongst the many critics of Bishop Alexander; who had been suspected of regularly breaking his obligation to celibacy and of much more, by sleeping with female members of his congregation; even with married women. When it was revealed that the College of Consultors had promoted him to Archbishop and the new Metropolitan of the Lagos Archdiocese, John was amongst the many members of the Clergy who had questioned his ability to handle such a position of power, given his lascivious past, and now, here John was, going to seek the permission of Archbishop Alexander, so that he could have the love of a woman; so that he could be released from his own obligation of celibacy.

They reach their destination and the taxi drives off the road, into the cathedral compound. The church vehicles had been occupied with various duties this morning, so Father John had decided to take a taxi to his meeting with the Archbishop. He pays the driver and steps out of the taxi, clutching his Bible and wearing his casual priestly clothing; black pants, black shoes, black button-up shirt and a white dog-collar.

The wind bouncing off the high building brushes past him as he approaches the cathedral. There are three arched doorways leading into the white-walled church, with the central arch rising the highest. These three arches also represent the three-fold responsibilities of the Church; proclaiming the word of God, celebrating the sacraments and exercising the ministry of charity. John enters the building with humility in his heart and heads for the parish office.

He does not have the luxury of considering himself more righteous than any member of the Clergy, anymore. Still, he is at peace with God because he did not conceal his sin, he brought it before the Lord. It has become common practice for many members of the Clergy to commit sin and, instead of repenting and confessing, continue to do so in secret. Since they are constantly under scrutiny from the Laity, they only have two choices; to live an exemplary life or to pretend to do so. John decided to take the third option; he decided it was best to lay down the responsibilities and extricate himself from the scrutiny of the Laity; he decided he wanted Aisha's love more than he wanted the Priesthood.

He enters the office of the Archbishop and is greeted by a deacon, who functions as his secretary.

"Good morning, Father," says the deacon, standing and smiling cordially.

"Good morning, Deacon," says John, returning his smile, "I'm Father John, here to see the Most Reverend Father Alexander."

"I believe he is expecting you, Father?"

"Yes, he is."

"Okay, Father. Please have a seat and I will let him know you are here."

"Thank you very much, Deacon."

John takes a seat while the deacon goes into the Archbishop's inner office. He prepares himself for all the words that will be exchanged. He hopes to speak less and listen more; he is willing to repudiated, in humility, like the wise King Solomon advised, in the Book of Proverbs, but at the end of the day he will stand by his decision.

*****

It's eleven p.m. on Friday night and Abu is seated at the back of a black SUV, along with three other men, armed with automatic rifles. He has been working with the Mustapha's for a year now and he has to come to understand their sacred position in the Nigerian Muslim community. He has come to understand the great responsibility vested on his shoulders by guarding the Emir of Kano's daughter.

The man seated beside Abu, at the back of the car, is loading extra bullets into the rifle magazines, as they drive over the Ikoyi bridge, heading towards Falomo, where the Church of Assumption is located. The other two men in front remain quiet, as they keep their eyes open for any police checkpoints. Abu is not armed today but on a few occasions like this, he has handled his own rifle. He is riding along with these three today, for other reasons.

He had left Nuru at home, in the staff quarters of the Mustapha residence and told him he was going to visit his family urgently, after they had brought the family back from the Nikah reception. He received his orders while he was still at the wedding but he had to wait to drop Karida, Kabiru and Aisha at home before doing as his employer had commanded him. He was not supposed to let anyone know about the mission, not even Nuru who he works closely with.

They park the black SUV, just outside the compound of the Church of Assumption, at Falomo, Ikoyi. The man who drove, turns back towards Abu, who is seated in the owner's corner.

"So, you can point him out, right? We have to make sure we get the right guy."

"No problem at all, I know the 'Pastor John' very well."

CHAPTER 10

"Let me read a few verses from the Book of Proverbs, between chapters six and nine," Archbishop Alexander Williams says, seated behind his desk, with a large leather-bound Bible beneath him.

"That would be delightful, most reverend Father. I was just reflecting on the Book of Proverbs, this morning," Father John replies, with his Bible placed on his laps, seated opposite the Metropolitan. It's about fifteen minutes past eleven a.m., on a Friday.

"Hmmm… the Spirit is one with us," Father Alexander hums, as he flips through the pages of the Bible. "I'll read a short passage first; chapter nine, verses thirteen to eighteen:

> "A foolish woman is clamorous;
>   she is simple, and knows nothing.
> For she sits at the door of her house,

on a seat in the high places
of the city,
to call those who pass by
who go right on their way:
"Whoever is simple, let him
turn in here."
And as for him who lacks
understanding, she says to
him,
"stolen waters are sweet,
and bread eaten in secret
is pleasant."
But he does not know that
the dead are there,
and that her guests are in
the depths of the grave."

John is familiar with these Bible verses and gradually begins to assume the direction in which their conversation would lean. It is false for the Archbishop to categorize a soul as pure as Aisha's with that of a foolish woman. Her actions towards him are not motivated by foolish desire but by love.

"Let us take a few more verses from chapter seven, of the same Book. Verses thirteen to twenty-three:

'She took hold of him and
kissed him
and with a brazen face she
said:
"Today I fulfilled my vows,

and I have food from my
fellowship offering at home.
So, I came out to meet you;
   I looked for you and have
found you!
I have covered my bed
   with colored linens from
Egypt.
I have perfumed my bed
   with myrrh, aloes and
cinnamon.
Come, let's drink deeply of
love till morning;
   let's enjoy ourselves with
love!
My husband is not at home;
   he has gone on a long
journey.
He took his purse filled with
money
   and will not be home till
full moon."
With persuasive words, she
led him astray;
   she seduced him with her
smooth talk.
All at once he followed her
   like an ox going to the
slaughter,

like a deer stepping into a
noose
  till an arrow pierces his
liver,
like a bird darting into a
snare,
  little knowing it will cost
him his life.'

John is also familiar with the last few verses read and he begins to wonder how much the Archbishop had heard about his relationship with Aisha. Did he know Aisha was betrothed to another man? Certainly, he had the wrong idea if he thought Aisha was a seductress or that it was lust that had led him here.

"I have one more verse to read and I will save that for last," says Father Alexander, as he finally brings his face up and looks directly at John. He wears a gentle smile, almost of admiration. "I have always seen a faithful person in you, Father John. I wish I could say you remind me of myself but that would not be true. I had my chance to be where you are now but my love was not strong enough; not as strong as yours..."

John can't tell where the conversation is leading but he is certainly less guarded towards the Archbishop. He had come ready with all the weapons of his heart, to defend his position and his request.

"I have been called many things, by the Laity and by the Clergy..." Father Alexander continues, "and sadly, most of those things were true. I broke my vow of celibacy and engaged in sexual affairs with many women... once or twice, I fell in love but I was not faithful enough to spend the rest of my life with either of them. You see, I came to learn that I was a slave to my lust in those days. Even when I did fall in love, I still gave into my lust and ruined the relationship..."

John listens reverently. He knows Archbishop Alexander must really respect him, to confer such delicate information upon him. Up until now, these things were just rumors to him but now he was confirming them.

"What I'm saying is, it is not a sin to fall in love and it is not a sin to marry. The sin is fornication, adultery and being a slave to your lust. Seeking a voluntary Laicization is the right thing to do, when you discover you have fallen in love and want to spend the rest of your life with a woman. The wrong thing to do, is to engage in sexual affairs with this woman, without a concrete plan to marry her; to hide your sins and continue in them... like I did. I was lured away by many desires and there was no shortage of women to express them with. It is not difficult to commit sin; it is difficult to stay righteous. The Lord Jesus said, 'if your right eye offends you, gouge it out because it is better to enter the Kingdom of Heaven with one eye...' in the same vein, Apostle Paul told Timothy that 'it is better to marry than to burn in hell.' So, you see, making a great change to your life, so that you can appear blameless before God, is a good thing. You are taking the necessary steps, to avoid a life of fornication and adultery. Your Parish Priest told me that you have not had any sexual encounters with this woman?"

"That is true, Most Reverend Father," John confirms. He then says; "but we have kissed."

"Hmmm… indeed you love for her is admirable. Tell me about this love you feel for her."

John's face suddenly lights up, with a growing smile. "I… have loved Aisha for years now. I had given up on the love, and that's when I joined the Convent… but now I've been given a second chance to be with her… she means everything to me. Loving her makes me feel closer to God; closer to my purpose on earth."

"The only thing I see as an obstacle for you, is her religion." Father Alexander says, sternly now. "I was told she is a Muslim. You do know that the Catholic church does not recommend a union with a Muslim. Are her parents in consent of her marrying a Catholic?"

"We are working towards telling her father but her mother is in consent," John replies. He then cautiously adds, "you should know, Most Reverend Father, also, that her father is the Emir of Kano."

"Wow," drops the Archbishop, with his mind envisioning various possibilities. "What a coincidence… that the one you love is the one you should not have. You don't think her father is going to welcome you with opens arms, do you?"

John is not sure how to respond. He certainly doesn't want to turn this into an argument, so he keeps quiet.

"I foresee… a lot of trouble ahead for you," continues Father Alexander, "I am confident that the love you have for this Aisha is real but you have also opened yourself to a great struggle; a struggle that started way before you were born; a struggle between Christianity and Islam. Hopefully, you would come out victorious. You did say that the love you feel for her makes you feel closer to your purpose. Maybe this struggle is your purpose but it is quite ominous that her father is the leader of an Islamic Sultanate."

"I do feel troubled in my spirit and the more I think on it, the more I am led towards fear," John says, unburdening his worries, "however, the Holy Spirit teaches that we have not fear in us but love, courage and a sound mind, so I constantly cast my fears away and focus on the love I feel."

"Certainly, the Holy Spirit is all you need. He will guide you through the mysteries... I will give my recommendation, for your Laicization, but I fear it may not be enough, when discovered that she is a Muslim and an Emir's daughter. Still, I will advise you to do that which will make you serve God with happiness in your heart, all the days of your life. That is the right thing to do."

"Thank you, Most Reverend Father. I appreciate your wisdom... how about the last verse, from the Proverbs?" John asks, curious, before leaving.

"Yes, emmm..." he flips a few pages through the Bible on his desk. "Here it is:

> 'He who finds a wife, finds a
> good thing and obtains favor
> from the Lord.'

Proverbs, chapter eighteen..." trails the Archbishop.

*****

The Nikah ceremony is taking place at the private residence of the Alhaji Dajani. There are hundreds of people in attendance, all dressed in their best traditional attires. Aisha is seated beside her mother and brother, on the bride's side. Her mother is seated right beside the mother of the bride; Alhaja Habibat Dajani.

The officiant for the wedding is a well-respected member of the bride's family and he is reciting the Khutba Nikah; the marriage sermon. All the Muslims listen reverently as he recites the opening text, from the Hadith:

> 'Praise be to Allah, we seek His help and His forgiveness. We seek refuge with Allah from the evil of our own souls and from our bad deeds. Whomsoever Allah guides will never be led astray, and whomsoever Allah leaves astray, no one can guide. I bear witness that there is no God but Allah, and I bear witness that Muhammad is His slave and Messenger'."

He then says in Arabic: "I seek refuge in Allah from the rejected and accursed Satan." He concludes the statement with: "Bismillah, Al-rahman, Al-raheem," before preparing to read the required verses from the Qur'an. He goes ahead to start the readings, with the Surah Al-nisa 4:1.

Karida Mustapha is filled with joy, watching her best friend's daughter get married. A part of her wants to wish that her daughter will also get married through a Muslim ceremony, just like this one, but she has come to terms with the fact; that wish will never come true, not after all Aisha has expressed to her. Her daughter made it clear to her that she is no longer interested in marrying Hassan and that she is in love with a Christian man. To top it off, not just any Christian man but a Catholic Priest.

While raising her only daughter, she instilled some lessons in her; about finding love and about finding happiness. She wanted her daughter to be amongst the new generation of Muslim women, who would not have to struggle for their freedom. Still, she ensured that Aisha took the Islamic law to heart and that she never strayed away from Allah, and from his Messenger. On a day like today, she wishes that she had been a little stricter with her daughter, maybe then she wouldn't have the courage to tell her mother that she wanted to marry a Catholic; maybe she would have obeyed her father's wishes and just married Hassan Ibrahim.

Karida knows what she saw in her daughter's eyes this week; it confirmed that it was something special she felt for this John. She can only claim to have felt that for her husband; Aliu Mustapha, six years after they got married. It was so inspiring to see it in her daughter's eyes, even before she had gotten married. It was similar to the look of a mother defending her child; it meant that Aisha had already endeared this John to her heart so much that she was willing to suffer for him. Karida didn't have the luxury of being in love with Aliu before she married him. She knew he was a kind and responsible man, and she was willing to take a chance with him. It was years later, after their third child, Usman, that she began to love him. It was then that she was willing to go through anything for him; to give her last dime to protect his interests. A powerful bond was then created.

If Aisha could feel this way about someone before they even knew each other sexually, then it was worth considering, even if this John was a Catholic. Deep down Karida felt relieved that he was a Priest. One thing she disdained about the Christians was their excessive liberty, which always gave rise to indiscipline and lasciviousness. This John, however, was a Priest and this meant he would have more self-discipline than the regular Christian and probably he would keep his vows to her daughter sacrosanct.

She had planned to meet with Pastor John last night, before the Nikah this morning, but instead she settled for a phone call with him. It was good to put a voice to the name but Karida was most interested in letting him know how much her daughter meant to her.

*****

Aisha was seated on her mother's king-size bed, with ribbons and wrapping paper scattered around her. She and Karida were wrapping gifts for the bride and groom at the Nikah tomorrow. Karida had taken it upon herself to please her best friend, Alhaja Habibat Dajani, on her daughter's wedding day. She had requested military personnel to be present at the Dajani's residence tomorrow, to help with security. She had also hired a second set of caterers, aside from the caterers hired by the Dajani's, to ensure that the guests at the event had a variety of food to choose from. Finally, she had lavished on a few gifts for the new couple; she bought a set of diamond earrings for the bride, along with luxury fabrics from Saudi Arabia, a twenty-four-karat gold watch for the groom, in addition to numerous kitchen appliances for their new home.

"Did you tell Kabiru I wanted to see him?" Karida asked her, while setting the luxury purple lace material in the wrapping paper, well cut-out by Aisha.

"He just got back in, so I asked one of the maids to let him know you're expecting him," Aisha replied, while carefully cutting out ribbons with a pair of scissors, to garnish the wrapped-up presents.

"I hope she delivers the message..." jeered Karida.

"Let me go and check again?" Aisha said, dropping the scissors and preparing to stand off the bed.

"No, sit. I'm sure she will," Karida said, stretching a hand to touch Aisha's thigh. "So... I said I wanted to meet John and you haven't made that possible, why?"

Aisha was taken aback. "Tonight?" she asked, stealing a look at the time on her phone, beside her: it was just a couple of minutes past eight.

"It would have been nice."

"I know you've been so busy with the Nikah. I didn't want to distract you."

"Distract me?" Karida asked, considering her eyes, "you've already distracted me with this news... now we have to focus on it. I want you to be happy, Aisha, but we are all servants of Allah and we must put Him first. If this is something that is going to happen, then we must do it in righteousness. We must seek the approval of your father. His consent can make everything possible because he is a part of the Islamic authority... but first, I need to speak my mind to this John, before I go ahead to risk my neck presenting this to your father."

"Should I ask him to... come over?" Aisha asked, finding it hard to swallow her saliva.

"It's already late. Let me speak to him on the phone. Call him."

Aisha was still finding it hard to collect her thoughts but she went ahead to pick her phone. "Okay." She pulled up his number and dialed it. There was a knock on the door and then it opened. Kabiru pushed the door slightly and popped his head in.

"You asked for me?" he asked, with a humble look.

"Yes, I want to discuss the soldiers you got from the barracks… but come back in fifteen minutes," his mother said, giving him her eyes, as the ringing tone was heard through Aisha's phone.

"Okay," Kabiru said and shut the door behind him.

"Hello, John, hi…" Aisha spurted into the phone. Her mother stretched out her hand, demanding the phone. Aisha handed it over without another word.

"Hello, John. This is Alhaja Karida speaking; Aisha's mother."

"Good… evening, ma. It's lovely to speak to you," John said cautiously, over the phone.

"My daughter tells me you have gotten her tangled in between your fingers."

"Oh, wow!" John breathed out. "It is probably the other way around."

"I wish it was neither," Karida said sternly. "I am not the type to segregate and neither did I teach my daughter to be that way, but you must admit that you are making our life uncomfortable by coming into it."

John was slightly hurt by her words but he looked beyond that, to her point. "You are right," he let out.

"If it makes my daughter's life more fulfilled, I will be willing to endure this discomfort… and you should know that coming into our lives might make yours also uncomfortable… do I need to elaborate or do you understand me?"

"I understand you fully. You have said all that needs to be said."

"I still have more to say," Karida charged on, "I can already sense that you have wisdom and honesty in you. So, I will ask you this once; are you ready to stick to my daughter, no matter what happens?"

A short silence. John was expecting a more difficult question. He then quickly spilled out the obvious answer. "Yes… I am hers."

Karida took a few seconds, to replay his answer in her head, to confirm if he meant and understood what he said. She couldn't help but feel at rest.

*****

It always gives Karida joy to give people things and especially, precious things. It is something that brings her closer to Allah. She had sent Kabiru to give the bride and the groom the gifts from the Mustapha family, after the Nikah had officially ended, and it was time to congratulate the groom. She and Aisha are helping to coordinate the caterers, while Kabiru has also been charged with keeping the military security organized. Her son Usman couldn't make it to the wedding because he had to be out of the country but his wife is here, with their son; Karida's grandson.

Karida always feels that she can do more for the world around her. She doesn't want to live a life without leaving a mark on people's hearts. Giving people things is her own way of connecting with them. She is grateful to Allah for being born into a wealthy family and to have also been married to a wealthy man, so she is always looking for avenues to touch other people's hearts, with gifts and gestures of love. Maybe that is why she has never had to lack; maybe it's like the Qur'an says; 'whatever you spend in good, it will be repaid to you in full, and you shall not be wronged.'

It is past four p.m. and the Walima; the wedding reception, has long begun. The attendants of the Nikah were moved to the large backyard of the Dajani's compound.

There are a few more people attending the Walima, who weren't at the Nikah. The bride and groom have already signed their marriage contract and the Mahr; the mandatory payment, has been given to the bride.

As soon as the Walima started, Karida came with her daughter, to join the caterers, to start with the distribution of food, while Kabiru went to tend to the security. Now, everybody has gotten settled down, the entertainment is going on modestly and the food and drinks are in full circulation. Karida gets pulled into a daydream as she stares at Habibat's daughter, seated at the front of the crowd, looking beautiful in her red and white, laced dress, and the henna designs craftily tattooed on her hands.

"Aisha!" exclaims a young lady, to Karida's daughter, smiling brightly.

"Ijeoma!!" Aisha exclaimed in return, lunging towards her long-time friend and opening her arms for a hug. Ijeoma, who appears equally excited, hugs her back. "You're here!" Aisha expresses, satisfied.

"Good evening, ma," Ijeoma says to Karida, "I thought, for a second, that Aisha was standing beside her sister."

Karida blushes and laughs shyly. "Hello Ijeoma. Thank you. It's been a while since I've seen you."

"It's not my fault, ma. We have Aisha to blame for that – she abandoned me."

"Oh, stop it!" Aisha cuts in. "We're here now, anyway."

"How are Amina and…"

"Funke – they're fine," Ijeoma adds, "I haven't seen them in a while. I know Amina is married now."

Aisha puts her hand in Ijeoma's and then turns towards her mother. "Mom, I'll be back shortly, let me gist with her – I'll seat close by, so call me if you need me."

"Okay, dear. Don't be too long." Karida says, releasing her. She then gives a final smile to Ijeoma, as they head towards an empty table, close by.

Aisha is quite happy to see Ijeoma, even more than she thought she would when they spoke on the phone. Maybe it's because it's a happy day or maybe it's because Ijeoma is the only person who might understand, apart from her mother, how she loves John. She can't deny, she is eager to tell Ijeoma all about the prospects of her rediscovered love.

"You missed the Nikah," Aisha says, scolding, as they get to a table.

"You know me, I can be fashionably late," Ijeoma taunts, as they take a seat. "Actually, I had to work because today is a Friday. Not everyone is a C E O like you."

"Oh, shush! I'm not C E O yet – maybe, one day."

"Babe, I almost turned back when I saw the soldiers outside with bazookas. Is this a war zone or something?"

Aisha lets out a giggle. "Bazookas indeed. It's my mom that brought the security o! Just to ensure the party goes smoothly – did you see Kabiru?"

"No…" Ijeoma stutters, remembering she can't be too honest with her friend. "Why do you ask?"

"Why not? I remember you used to have a crush on him."

Ijeoma chuckles. "That was then... it didn't work out... and I haven't been in touch with him. I'm sure... he is planning to get married to his fiancé now."

"Well, he is," Aisha retorts, dropping the topic.

"How about your fiancé? Hassan..." Ijeoma tries to drive the conversation in her desired direction, "very soon, it's your Nikah I'll be coming to, right?"

Aisha hesitates to give a response, even though she is eager to speak. "Well... I am quite sure I won't be marrying Hassan but I hope to get married soon."

"Oh, really? What happened between you guys?"

"...nothing. I just... found love, again. You remember John?"

"John, from Unilag?" Ijeoma asks.

"Yeah... don't tell anyone, yet, but I got back together with him and we're... working towards getting married."

"Wooow... so you've broken it off with Hassan?"

"Not yet," Aisha says, cautiously, "I've just told my mom – it's only been less than a month since I reconnected with John – I plan to tell my dad soon and then... it's a bit complicated – John is now a Catholic Priest, so he also needs to release himself from his obligations."

"Catholic Priest? John? What church? I'm a Catholic too."

"The Church of Assumption, Ikoyi."

"Wow… but… how would your parents ever agree to you marrying a Catholic?" Ijeoma asks, curious. "Don't you think it's a little… crazy?"

"It is crazy… I guess love is that way. I just… want to be with him and he wants the same thing. You of all people should understand – you once liked my brother. Don't you wish there was nothing standing in between?"

"Sure, I do – I mean, I did but your father is now the Emir of Kano. How would you explain it to him?"

"Gradually, I guess. My mom is already behind me and she'll find a way to open the conversation."

"Hmmm… I think you should tell Hassan, as soon as possible," Ijeoma advises, seeing a silver lining, "break it off with him, so you can quench his expectations."

"…you're right. I guess I have been avoiding that but it's because I don't want my father to hear about it the wrong way. I want to control the news for now… so, don't tell anyone yet."

"Who do I want to tell?" Ijeoma asks, already feeling guilty.

"Maybe Kabiru – don't look, he's on his way here," Aisha lowers her voice and puts her palm over Ijeoma's,

"...probably to talk to you – I'll be back, let me check on my mom. Don't go anywhere."

"Okay," Ijeoma says. Aisha gets up from the table just before Kabiru reaches them.

"Don't go, I was coming to see you," he calls to Aisha as she leaves.

"Sure, you were," Aisha jeers, walking away. Kabiru turns to Ijeoma, taken aback, wondering what they'd been talking about.

"Play along," Ijeoma whispers to him, "sit down and act like you were coming to see me."

Kabiru smiles, then sits down opposite her, in full view of his mother. "I was coming to tell her that the soldiers needed a second round of food and drinks, and then maybe say hello to you in a casual way."

"Well, I guess this is plan B." She looks him in the eyes, coldly. He looks back at her, aloof.

"So, what were you girls talking about? Has she spoken about John?"

"Yeah, she's told me everything you need to know but, fortunately, there is nothing you can do with the information."

"What do you mean?"

"She is not having an affair. She is planning to marry John. She said she is going to call it off with Hassan soon.

Secondly, 'Father John' is now a catholic Priest, at the Church of Assumption, which makes him beyond your reach. He most likely lives in the church rectory, along with other members of Clergy, so unless you want to start a war or a riot, you wouldn't dare think of laying a finger on him. He is planning to leave the Priesthood soon, just to marry your sister... I think you should reconsider whose side you're on. Think of your sister's happiness. Hassan's jealousy is none of your business."

"She can't marry a catholic. She's not marrying John," Kabiru growls.

"Well, your mom has agreed; she's just waiting to tell your father."

"That's ridiculous." He throws an incredulous look towards Aisha and Karida.

"Whatever, just keep your mouth shut," Ijeoma scolds, "you know the only reason why I did this was because of the bond between us; because I love you, and the only reason why you believed I would do it was because you know I love you... don't dare take that for granted. You're not telling anyone what I told you, especially not Hassan; that's final. Sort it out with your sister," she concludes.

Kabiru takes a while to digest the information, while trying to keep a calm demeanor because of his mother who's close by. Luckily Ijeoma is backing her and Aisha, so they can't see the embittered expression on her face.

"You should go now. I think that's enough catchup. We're only pretending, aren't we?" she spills, looking away from him. He tries to catch her eyes once more before getting up but she keeps them away from him.

"See you soon," Kabiru says over her shoulder, as he heads towards his mother.

*****

Abu's heart races, with adrenaline, as the military-trained man beside him inserts loaded magazines into two handy, Heckler and Koch MP5K machine guns. There are three other people in the black SUV but the driver; Danlami, is the only person Abu is familiar with, because they were both trained at same time, through their secondary school level, in the Nigerian military academy. Abu didn't further his education, like Danlami, but instead started working as a bodyguard and driver.

"We have to go in and get what we want, in fifteen minutes, max," Danlami instructs, pulling out his silver 44-Magnum Revolver pistol, from beneath his driver's seat, "ten minutes would be better. Sharp-sharp, in and out."

"Sure," consents Abu.

The fourth man, at the backseat, passes one of the loaded MP5 rifles to the man in the front passenger seat.

"You don't think I need a piece?" Abu asks Danlami, trying to prove his mettle to the other two.

"We're not going to kill anybody, except it's necessary," Danlami says, reaching over to the passenger seat, to the glove compartment of the car, "but you can carry my Triple-O knife." He pulls out a heavy retractable knife and hands it to Abu.

"This is okay," Abu says, collecting the knife. He pushes a button on the handle and the sharp blade springs out. He pushes the button again and the blade is retracted back into the handle.

The guy seated beside Abu pulls out four black scarfs from a brown backpack beside him, which is also carrying extra bullets. He throws one scarf to everyone in the car. Abu, knowing what to do, ties the scarf securely over his nose and around the lower back of his head. He then pulls the scarf down, under his chin. The others have tied their scarves securely also, ready to cover their faces when they enter the church premises.

Danlami steps out of the Black SUV first, wearing thick black jeans and a baggy, long sleeve, dark brown, button-down shirt. He picks up his 44-Magnum pistol from his seat, stealthily sticks it under the back of his shirt and tucks it in between his leather belt and trouser waistband.

"Magaji, these traditional clothes you're wearing, for this operation?" Danlami complains, just as Magaji motions to open the front passenger door.

"This one will not disturb," Magaji replies, taking another look at his black Dashiki, made of Kaftan fabric, with matching pants, and leather slippers. He then throws a look towards the backseat, at the fourth man in the SUV. "The same thing Rabiu is wearing," he protests.

"Anyhow, just package your guns," Danlami concludes, shutting the driver's door. Rabiu pulls out two black, poly-woven sacks and hands one to Magaji. They both insert their small-sized MP5 rifles into the black sacks and hold the sacks by the cut-out handles.

Abu steps down from the back, wearing dark-blue, khaki pants and a dark-grey hoodie. He sticks his Triple-O knife in the large pockets of his hoodie and then shuts his door, taking a deep breath of cold night-air.

*****

It's less than an hour to the midnight Vespers and deacon Benedict is on his way out of the Church of Assumption compound, to get himself and deacon Babatunde some Suya from the Hausa man who sells, just across the road. Babatunde had given five hundred Naira to Benedict, to help him get an adequate amount of the roasted, peppered meat.

Benedict has been a deacon for almost three months now, hoping to be a Priest soon. Within a few months or more, he would be eligible to join the Priesthood, but he would still have to wait for a member of the Priesthood to die or retire before he would get ordained. With the news of Father John about to leave the Priesthood, he can't deny, his hopes have been taken up; the door might just be opened for him but it is never worth celebrating, when a member of the Priesthood abandons his obligations, so Benedict has chosen to keep his hopes to himself.

He greets the gateman as he passes through the open pedestrian gate, "good evening, Richard."

"Good evening, deacon Benedict," Richard muffles, from within the gatehouse, in between munching down on his dinner; Jollof rice, with a few chunks of beef and fried plantain, which he bought from a nighttime hawker.

Four men pass by Benedict as he stands at the edge of the main road, waiting to cross, and they head into the church, through the pedestrian gate. Two of them are dressed in black and dark brown Dashikis, holding black poly-woven sacks. The other two behind them are dressed in casual clothing. For some reason, their demeanor makes deacon Benedict feel troubled in his spirit. He keeps his eyes on all four of them, as they enter the compound. He seems to recognize one of the men; the one wearing dark-blue pants and a dark-grey hoodie. He might have come to the church once or twice but he is certainly not a regular member.

The man at the rear, wearing jeans and a button-down shirt, enters last and goes straight into the gatehouse, while the other three stand aside, waiting. They all pull up black scarfs over their faces and then he sees, through the gatehouse window louvers, the man in jeans pull out a silver-colored gun and point it at Richard; the gateman.

Benedict quickly crosses the road, struck with fear. He tries his best to act casual, so he doesn't draw the attention of the four men.

He disregards the Hausa man selling Suya and pulls out his mobile phone from his pocket, as soon as he gets across the road, but it falls to the ground, out of his shaking hand, and the battery pops out. He gathers the pieces of his dismantled device and walks further away, while trying frantically to reassemble the pieces. His first thought is to call the police.

*****

Danlami approaches the gateman, pointing his 44-Magnum, with his black scarf over his nose. "If you make any noise!"

"No noise, no noise, sir," Richard replies. Danlami rests his pistol on his chest. He then looks around for the light switch. He quickly flicks it, so people passing by cannot see him. "This is a church, sir," Richard pleads, confused, "we don't have anything here."

"Shut up. Where are the priests staying?" Danlami asks, pressing the pistol into his chest.

"They are in the rectory, sir," Richard reveals.

Danlami gives him a heavy slap with his left hand, while still holding the gun to his chest. "Get up! Take us there – up!" he commands.

Richard carefully gets up, scared to death of the pistol pressed into his chest. Danlami lowers the gun and then presses it into the gateman's waist, just above his left buttocks. Richard proceeds out of the gatehouse, with his legs shaking. He passes by the other three men, with their faces covered under black scarves; two holding poly-woven sacks.

He walks slowly across the church building, while Danlami and the other three, follow closely behind.

"Will you move fast!" Danlami threatens, poking Richard sharply with the barrel of his pistol. Richard, intoxicated with fear, starts to trot.

"Yes, sir," he replies, pleading. The four men pick up their pace behind him. Magaji and Rabiu pull out their rifles and drop the black poly-woven sacks on the ground. Abu follows, with his eyes darting around the compound for any witnesses, and his hand clutching the tactical knife in his hoodie pocket.

They go around the church building and head directly towards the rectory. Richard turns his head back to point out the building to Danlami but he is horrified to see two machine guns in the hands of the other men, who were holding poly sacks some seconds ago. He panics, and in a surge of fear, starts to run towards the rectory, with all the strength he can muster.

"Thief! Ole! Robbers! Ole!" Richard screams as he bolts inside the rectory. Danlami sprints after him, being a much faster runner. Richard throws himself into the rectory and runs across the central hallway, straight for the Parish Priest's room. The rectory is a bungalow building with a central hallway, dividing a set of eight small rooms, with a ninth master bedroom at the end of the hallway. "Ole! Ole! Thief!" Richard continues to scream within the rectory, throwing panic into the inhabitants.

Danlami is about seven steps behind him. He enters the rectory, stops and aims his 44-Magnum Revolver pistol at Richard. He pulls the trigger sending a bullet into Richard's thigh. Richard falls and shrieks, just as he reaches the Parish Priest's door, but still manages to bang the door twice with his fist.

Two doors open along the hallway and two deacons step out, trying to figure out what is going on. The sounds of two other doors being locked can be heard.

Magaji, Rabiu and Abu step into the rectory hallway also. The two deacons raise up their hands as they see the weapons in the hands of the strangers.

"Everybody out!" Danlami commands, blaring across the hallway. Rabiu and Magaji point their guns at the two deacons and approach them. The master bedroom is heard to be unlocked and the Parish Priest; Father Aderemi Etomi steps out, wearing a black Cassock.

"Peace be unto you," he says humbly to Danlami, sensing he was in charge.

"Is that Pastor John?" Danlami asks Abu.

"No," Abu replies, holding out the Triple-O blade.

"Where is Pastor John? Produce him and we will leave peacefully, if not your people will suffer."

"Please, may I ask; what has he done?" Father Aderemi enquires cautiously.

"He is a harlot and we are going to punish him according to our law," Danlami announces, "hand him over."

"Deacon Babatunde," calls the Parish Priest to one of the men who stepped out, "where is Father John?"

"He... he left about thirty minutes ago. I don't... know where," Babatunde stammers, with Magaji's rifle pointed closely at him. He receives a slap.

"Makàryàcī! Liar!" Magaji exclaims before giving him a second slap.

"I wouldn't lie, sir, he left. You can check his room," Babatunde pleads, holding his right cheek with both hands.

"Everybody out!!" Danlami roars, banging his left fist on one of the doors that was heard to be locked.

Three doors are unlocked. The assistant Parish Priest steps out and two other deacons. Rabiu leaves the first two deacons under Magaji's control and approaches the others slowly, pointing his rifle towards them."

"Everybody, for center!" Rabiu commands.

"You too!" Danlami yells at Father Aderemi. The Parish Priest leaves the bleeding gateman and walks across the hallway, towards the other members of Clergy. They all congregate around each other, shivering with fear. The Parish Priest tries his best to put up a calm demeanor.

"Kneel down! Everyone!" Danlami commands. The two priests and four deacons kneel, in the center of the hallway. "Is Pastor John here?" Danlami asks Abu.

"No," Abu replies.

"Check all the rooms," Danlami tells Rabiu, while he and Magaji keep their guns pointed at the six men.

Rabiu quickly goes through the open rooms first, starting with the Parish Priest's. The rooms are modestly furnished with just a bed and a reading table. He checks underneath all the beds and within all the wardrobes. He then begins to kick down the doors of the remaining three rooms. He checks within those but does not find anyone.

"No one," Rabiu asserts firmly.

"I will ask only once," Danlami says to Father Aderemi, taking a step forward and grabbing deacon Babatunde by the collar. He shoves the barrel of his silver pistol down the deacon's mouth. "Where is Pastor John?"

"Please, sir, please. Don't shed any more blood on God's holy ground," the Parish Priest preaches, "I can assure you that Pastor John is not here, just like deacon Babatunde said; please, let him go."

"You bunch of harlots and homosexuals. What is Allah looking for on this ground?" Danlami slithers. He then knocks Babatunde on the head with the handle of his pistol, sending him slumping on the floor. "Let's go; time up," he announces to his three partners.

"Everyone, inside!" Magaji commands the members of the Clergy, pointing into one of the small rooms. They all get up and hurry in. The Parish Priest and one of the deacons drag Babatunde in, who's still unconscious.

"He needs a hospital, please," Father Aderemi begs Danlami, of Richard; the gateman.

"He's an idiot, let him bleed well. He's lucky I didn't shoot him in the head," replies Danlami, casting a murderous look at Richard, who's still on the floor at the far end of the hallway, bleeding in silence.

"Get inside!" Magaji says, giving the Parish Priest a heavy slap. The other members of clergy stare at Magaji incredulously, as Father Aderemi humbly enters the room.

He pulls out the key from the other side of the door and locks all six members of clergy inside the room.

"Sharp-sharp; out of here!" Danlami commands, as he tucks his revolver-pistol away. He takes long strides, out of the rectory and then across the church compound. The other three do the same. Magaji and Rabiu pick up their black poly-woven sacks, where they dropped them, and conceal their Heckler & Koch MP5K rifles.

*****

John is staring over the Lagos Lagoon and the Ikoyi suburbs, standing on the balcony of room nine-o-six, at the Lagos Oriental hotel, with Aisha. The stretched reflection of bright, yellow lights shimmer on the water's elastic surface.

The picturesque view is calming but he can't stop feeling troubled in his spirit; it's been that way for a week now. However, having Aisha beside himself, like he does now, gives him the courage to dare on.

It's eleven thirty-six as John's phone rings, from inside the hotel room.

Aisha walks into the room through the open glass doors, with wind-blown, light curtains. She pulls out John's ringing phone from her handbag on the table and hurriedly walks back, to hand it to him.

He collects it from her. "Thanks." He picks the call, "hello, Benedict?"

CHAPTER 11

John had finished his African History, General Studies exam, twenty minutes before it was time-up. Naturally, he would have gone home, to his uncle's house on campus, and avoided the arduous after-exam fraternizing, but he couldn't leave without testing his luck.

There were over three hundred students taking the General Studies exam, which meant there would be a flood of people pouring out of the exam hall as soon as it was over. He remained confident, that he would spot her red Hijab as soon as she walked out, and then he would get his chance to talk to her, and hopefully she would talk back. He had helped her out with her exam questions but he had come to learn, from three years of social life in the University of Lagos, that being nice to a pretty girl was not always enough to deserve her attention.

Something about her said she wasn't like every other pretty girl; she seemed modest and unpretentious. Maybe it was all in his head; maybe he was just fascinated by her mysterious eyes, but he was about to find out. It was time-up for everyone taking the exam and a few students began to trickle out of the three doors leading into the exam hall, while most of the others were still taking their time to submit their answer sheets.

And there she came, out of the middle door, with her red Hijab and black Abaya, sparkling in the mid-afternoon sunlight. His heart skipped a beat, not sure if to approach her in front of all those people but suddenly, she turned her eyes toward him, smiled, and changed her direction towards the notice boards, where he was standing. He couldn't see anyone but her; it was as though the picture of everyone else was blurred, while only she's was in focus. Her movement was steady and graceful, like she floated towards him, in her flowing Abaya.

"I don't know your name?" she threw, getting to him. He was wearing a black t-shirt and blue jeans.

"I'm John. How about you?"

"I'm Aisha... you... shouldn't have done what you did, really. I admit, I didn't have the answers to ninety percent of the questions but you just shouldn't have taken such a risk, not to mention, break the rules..."

John found himself feeling penitent but he was still confused because she seemed to have a smile on her face.

"...what I'm trying to say is; thank you for helping me – my senior brother got married yesterday, so I didn't have time to read. I guess... I owe you one, John."

"No, you don't," he corrects her, "I expect my reward – or punishment – from God. I was trying to help you pass, unlike I did when I took the exam the first time."

"You're not in hundred-level, are you?" Aisha asked, tilting her head, while looking at him.

"Nope, I'm in three-hundred."

"Well..." she sang, "I guess if God punishes you for your 'good deed', then we both fail and if he blesses you, we both pass, because I copied everything you wrote down." She laughed. He did too.

The crowd leaving the exam hall moved in a general direction, towards the cab park, where they could get a shuttle back to the faculty area. Only a few students in the University of Lagos had their faculties close to the large halls where exams like these were usually held.

The order of the day would be to get back to your faculty and read for your next exam, if you had a second paper that day, or loiter about if you had some free time.

"Is your faculty up-school?" John asked, insinuating that they take a shuttle together.

"Yeah, I'm studying Business Admin," she said, consenting and walking in the general direction, with the crowd. "You?"

"I'm studying Philosophy," he said, walking along with her. "Do you have another exam today?"

"No, I should be heading home soon... but it's a Saturday, so I might just hang around with my friends before leaving." She turned her face towards him, "why do you ask?"

"Well, nothing really, just wondering if you would have some time to spend with me."

"You want me to spend time with you? Why?" she asked, curious to understand his inclinations.

"Well, nothing really, just want to make a new friend," he responded, feeling interviewed.

"Oh my, the queue is so long!" Aisha exclaimed, getting to the cab park and seeing that a large part of the three hundred students who took the exam were waiting for the four-seater shuttles. She looked at John; he looked back.

"I hate queues; I'd rather walk the distance to my faculty," he contributed.

"Me too. Let's go."

"Okay." He followed her as she turned away from the cab park and towards the sidewalk of the main road, connecting the whole campus. "So, I get to spend time with you, great," he rejoices, comically

She chuckled. "Not so fast; you still haven't explained why you want my time," she said, as they moved along the treey sidewalk, "they say time is more precious than money, so why should I give you any?"

"So that I can learn about you. It takes time to do that."

"What do you want to learn about me?" she queried, almost defensively, "I don't tell strangers things about myself."

"I hope to stop being a stranger, so I will tell you everything about myself, first," he suggested, smiling, "and then, maybe if you find me 'worthy', you can tell me a few things about you."

She giggled. "Fine then. Go ahead, jabber away."

"Okay... so, I'm John Amaechi... I live on campus with my uncle; Professor Kevin Amaechi, who's also a lecturer in the Philosophy department... emmm... I studied Philosophy because of my uncle, as you can guess... I want to be a Lecturer too, one day or better yet, a Vice Chancellor; I feel education is something I want to be a part of... I'm an only-child... my parents are late, so I was sort-of adopted by my uncle, when I was sixteen –

"Both parents..." she rewound, consoling him, "wow, I'm sorry."

"Thanks. It's been over four years, so I've gotten over it now," he said, brushing away the weighty feelings.

"I see why you look up to your uncle a lot."

"Well..." he corrected her, "I admire and respect him but I don't want to be him."

"Why?"

"Because… he is lonely. He never got married and he spends most of his time all alone… I don't want to be so lonely."

Aisha took a moment to think. "Everybody needs someone… at least one," she said, staring at the ground wistfully.

"That's what I think too."

They walked along, both thinking in silence, and then she cut in; "so you live on campus; that must be fun?"

"Well, it's okay."

"Me, I'm always surrounded by my family and we don't go out much. It's the little time I spend in school that's a taste of freedom, and my brother is always close by, with the driver, to take me home before I get to discover much," she ended up blurting out. "What's the most beautiful place on campus?"

"Hmmm… that's easy; the Lagoon Front," he declared.

"I've heard of the Lagoon Front but I've never been there."

"Really? And you've spent almost a year in this school?" John taunted her.

"So, what? I'm still new and I just told you, I don't get much time to explore. I usually hang out with my friends; Ijeoma, Funke and Amina, and we just go to the cafeteria or the girl's hostels."

"Should I take you to the Lagoon Front?" he proposed, hoping she'd approve.

"Sure. It's one day I'll see it."

"You've been missing the wonderful scenery – do you know that the body of water you see under the third mainland bridge, is not the Atlantic Ocean? The same water that passes the Lagoon Front..."

"I didn't know that. I thought that was the Atlantic Ocean I was looking at, whenever we drove over the third mainland bridge," she replied, interested.

"Nope. That's the Lagos Lagoon," he continued expatiating, "it's quite big; it flows all the way past Ikosi, Ikorodu, to Ikoyi, Victoria Island and Ajah. It finally bursts into the Atlantic Ocean through Tarkwa Bay, but most of the water you see around Lagos is the same Lagos Lagoon, except of course, the beaches. The beaches are facing the Atlantic Ocean directly."

"Wow... so the Lagoon that passes by the University is the same one that stretches to Lekki, Phase-one, where I stay?" she enquired.

"Yep."

"Hmmm... I learnt something new; what a nice introduction to the Lagoon Front – you should be a tourist guide." They both chuckled. They walked along, still a while away from the scenic destination. She then turned to him. "So... I'm Aisha Mustapha... I live in Lekki, with my mom and dad, and my brothers..."

*****

John sticks the card-key into the door of room nine-o-six with his right hand, while holding a large nylon grocery bag his left hand. Aisha is beside him, standing in the hallway, holding a nylon grocery bag in each hand, with her handbag hung over her right shoulder. The key-light reads green, so he twists the knob, opening it. He stands aside for Aisha to go in first, before pulling out the card key, entering and shutting the hotel room door.

They had stopped by at the Buy-Right supermarket, to get a few toiletries, some snacks, drinks and other utilities. Aisha had come with her driver; Nuru, to pick John, just outside the church, so they could spend the night together.

She spent less than an hour at home, after the Nikah. She and John had been chatting via text and after experiencing the love-centered activities of the day, she knew she had to be with her own love, and she was thankful she had one. She asked him if he could be with her tonight and he consented.

After stopping by to get fast-food and then stopping by at the supermarket, they had decided to spend more than just a night together; they booked the Lagos Oriental Hotel room for a whole week. Karida and Kabiru were travelling back to Kano in the morning, so Aisha was, once again, going to be the only one at home, apart from the numerous staff and other members of her extended family, who live in other buildings within the compound.

Aisha drops the two nylon bags in her hands on the table in the room, as well as her handbag, and begins to look through the bags. John lets his single bag rest on the bed and pulls out toothbrushes, soap and toothpaste from it. He then walks into the bathroom to place them. Aisha pulls out a pack of juice and a bottle of water from one of the nylon bags, and opens the small fridge to place them inside. She then, from the same bag, pulls out ice cream, biscuits and chocolate bars, and places them in the fridge also.

"The burgers are already cold," Aisha whines, pulling out two take-away packs from the second nylon bag.

"If we call the kitchen, they should be able to get it warm for us," John suggests, as he approaches the table to drop his nylon bag.

"Yeah, they will," she replies, relieved. "Can you call them, please?"

"Okay." He heads back towards the bed to pick up the telecom phone on the bedside cabinet. He sits on the bed and dials the kitchen, while Aisha goes into the bathroom and shuts the door. "Hello," John says over the phone, "please we would like to warm some food. Can you send someone up? ...room nine-o-six... thank you."

He puts down the telecom and then stands up. He takes a second to consider the feelings in his spirit. He has been feeling extra-troubled ever since he got back from the meeting with the Archbishop this morning but he prayed to the Lord, by the worshipful intercession of His glorious Mother, and asked for help. He has learnt, through his years in the church, to never disregard the prodding of his spirit, but he is also confident that the Lord will protect and always lead him in the direction of the rising sun. His faith is strong, so he decides to continue in prayer, in his heart.

He walks towards the glass door leading to the balcony and opens it. He steps outside, brushed by the gushing wind. The wind then subsides, having found its way into the room, and John leans on the balcony railing. From his elevated position, he takes in the view of the Lagos island at night. He can almost see his church from the hotel and, of course, he can see the flowing waters of the Lagos Lagoon below.

"I want to spend all my time with you, John," comes Aisha as she steps onto the balcony and hugs him from behind. She buries her face into his back, just behind his chest, and she feels his heartbeat. "Do you remember what you asked me the first day we met?" she asks, as he turns around to face her.

"I asked a few questions, which?" He places his hands on her waist.

"You... kind-of asked if I had time to spend with you," she reminds him.

John giggles as he remembers. "Yes, so I could learn about you."

"Have you learnt enough now?" she asks, leaning her face close to his.

"No... I haven't," he says and then pecks her on the lips, "I want to learn every day; learning never stops." He closes his eyes and kisses her deeply. The heavy feeling in his spirit is lifted, even if temporarily, and once again he feels closer to his purpose; he feels closer to God.

They detach, smiling, and then both lean on the railing of the balcony, to take in the scenic view, keeping their bodies close together.

"I've decided, I'm going to go back to the University to teach – after I further my studies," he utters, from deep in his thoughts.

"Hmmm... sounds interesting. What would you teach?"

"Philosophy; it's what I always wanted to teach," he says, smiling, "the mother of all courses."

"Professor John Amaechi," she sings. He chuckles.

"It's going to be great being with you all week," he drops.

"I think it's going to be the best week of my life, yet," she beams, "coming back here from work and seeing you in the evening… can't wait."

"I'll have to go to the church frequently, even though I have already stepped down from most of my duties… but we'll spend the evenings together."

"Mornings too," she says holding his palm. The muffled sound of a ringing phone can be heard from inside the room. "I think your phone is in my handbag – let me get it."

She steps off the balcony and into the room. She retrieves John's phone from her bag and hurriedly heads back outside, to hand it to him. She had kept it for him when they were at the supermarket.

"Thanks," he says, collecting the phone from her. He recognizes the number before picking the call. "Hello, Benedict?"

"Hello, Father John, there has been an incident," Benedict's shaky voice comes, over the phone.

"What is the problem?"

"We were attacked by some Hausa men, probably terrorists – but they were looking for you, specifically. They shot Richard, our guard, in the thigh – he's been taken to the hospital – they came with guns –

"What?! Is anyone else hurt?" John is shaken. Aisha can sense the tension in his voice and she's struck with fear.

"Not really; they knocked Deacon Babatunde on the head but he is okay and they assaulted Father Aderemi and other deacons," Benedict blurts out.

"They were asking for me?" John asks, dumbfounded.

"Yes! I was lucky I was just heading outside the compound when they entered but I was told they were looking for Pastor John – I called the police but they got here late."

"I am on my way to the church."

"No, don't. Father Aderemi asked me to call you – he's talking with the police now – but he mentioned that you should stay where you are, just in case they come back."

"This is unbelievable... I'll be there in the morning then... I'm really sorry."

"I don't believe this is your fault, Father; this is the Devil's work. Please, stay out of sight, and see you in the morning. Peace be with you."

"Peace be with you, Deacon," John says, saddened. He brings down the phone.

"What happened, love?" Aisha asks, eager to know. John looks back at her but hesitates to respond. He doesn't know who could have been behind such an attack but he is wise enough to discern that it was all caused because he let himself fall in love with her again. He sensed the danger before he gave in. He can also discern that there is more trouble to come. Is he being selfish and blind by giving into his heart? How much trouble will come because he wants to be happy? Should he stop now and let her go?

He holds onto his faith and decides to share the problem with her. It's clear that he escaped the Devil tonight because he chose to be with her. "The church was attacked," he starts.

*****

Nuru drives Aisha along Adeola Odeku, through the slothful traffic, on their way to Vodasat Telecoms. It's some minutes to nine, on a Saturday morning, and the lazily-rising sun still has a golden glow.

Aisha is quietly seated at the owner's corner, with the windows wound up, and the TV screen, in the headrest in front her, turned on. She is watching the morning news, still dazed by the events of last night.

"Also frontpage news, on the Daily Clarion; 'Lagos Catholic church attacked by Boko Haram? – One shot and others injured, Assailants came looking for Priest; Father John.' Nkechi Ejiofor, the popular TV show host reads, on the Morning Catch-Up show. She holds up a newspaper, which has a picture of the church building, along with a smaller picture of John inserted below.

"This is the story of the day!" Kunle Adepoju, a co-host for the Morning Catch-Up show, blares across the TV, "what is Boko Haram's business with an assistant Parish Priest – or co-assistant? I believe this story is still unfolding; there is some hot pepper-soup about to be served."

"What do you think, Kemi?" Nkechi Ejiofor asks her second co-host, Kemi Adigun.

"I don't have enough to construct a... an informative thought, Nkechi. I just advise that we stay away from rumors at this point. Calling these group of assailants 'Boko Haram' is false and could lead to panic, you know..." Kemi lays out her thoughts patiently, "according to the reports I got from a source at the Ikoyi police station, the men were simply described as 'Hausa', and 'most likely Muslim'. There is no telling if it was a terrorist attack – not to mention they went there looking for a specific person; Father John, and when they didn't find him, they left. They only shot the gateman, who was said to have tried to escape."

"So, you think it could just be a personal feud with this 'Father John' and not directed at the whole religious institution?" Nkechi asks her.

"Exactly, Nkechi. I don't think this was a direct attack on the Christians — it's no Muslim-versus-Christian battle, and we definitely shouldn't let it degenerate into that. What we need to do is speak with 'Father John' and ask him what he has gotten himself involved with; he might have gotten his hands dirty; he might be owing the wrong person money."

"That is certainly a cautious line of thought —"

"Caution is not necessarily the solution here, Kemi," Kunle dives in, determinedly, "for all we know, these might just *be* terrorists — maybe not Boko Haram; maybe a new or unknown sect; and maybe not — but the elephant in the room that we cannot ignore, is the fact that this attack was carried out within a church. That, for me, is crossing the boundary between caution and chaos — that is desecrating a holy ground and insulting every Christian in the country, and beyond!" Kunle Adepoju emphasizes.

Aisha listens to the opinions attentively, knowing this all affects her directly. She is a lot more eager than they are, to discover the answer to this riddle.

"You're watching the Saturday Morning Catch-Up news, on Numbers Television. We'll be back in a few moments. Let's take a commercial break," Nkechi announces, while her co-hosts sit quietly.

Aisha turns off the TV in the headrest. She wonders who would want to hurt John but she can't deny the strong feeling that it's all connected to her.

"Where is Abu?" she asks Nuru, noticing the front passenger seat is empty.

"Yes, madam," Nuru replies, looking into the rear mirror, "After the Nikah, I think he went to his family's house; yesterday night."

"Okay," Aisha replies, thinking nothing of it. She pulls out her phone from her bag and fiddles with it.

After the phone call from the church, her night with John turned left, and all the budding joy was replaced with gloominess. John had left the hotel at about seven-thirty in the morning. Her mother and Kabiru had travelled back to Kano on the eight-a.m. flight, as they had planned

She's been quizzing her mind since last night; she knows she told her mother everything about John but she refuses to believe her empathetic mother could be behind such violence. Not even her father could do something so barbaric, being a protagonist of peace and a modern thinker – neither had her mother had the time to give him any details. The only person she suspects could be behind this, is Kabiru. Possibly Hassan, but she can't think of a way he could have found out without Kabiru being involved. Her thoughts lead her back to Kabiru; he was the one who shattered her happiness with John the first time, on her nineteenth birthday.

Honestly, she's finding it hard to believe that her brother could be involved in orchestrating an attack on a church but if he was, that would mean someone had told him about her relationship with John. It could have been

Karida but, most probably Ijeoma, because her mother had no reason to betray the confidence. Aisha feels a deep need to discover the truth, before it's too late.

She remembers telling Ijeoma everything about John, including the name of his Parish, and she knows Kabiru had spoken to her a few times at the Walima. She might have spilled it to him.

She decides to call Ijeoma and cautiously find out if her suspicions are leading to the truth. She pulls up her number and dials it.

The phone rings.   "Aishaaa," Ijeoma's voice sounds, delighted over the phone.

"Hi, dear," she ingratiates her, staring blindly out the car window, "you left without saying bye last night."

"Ah-ah, I was with you for over two hours and I saw you were getting busy with your mom – just say you miss me already," Ijeoma jibes.

She forces a giggle. "Maybe… have you seen the news this morning?"

"No, I haven't. What about the news?"

"There was an attack – some people with guns – at the Church of Assumption, Ikoyi…"

"Attack? Isn't that where… John…" Ijeoma trails.

"Yes… and the major shock is that the armed men went there *looking for* John. Luckily he was… somewhere else."

"Wow! What did they want with John?" Ijeoma asks, strangely distant.

"We don't know yet but it's all over the news, TV, newspapers – this morning, they're calling it a terrorist attack," Aisha says. She then breathes out before saying; "Ijeoma, I need you to tell me something; did you tell Kabiru about John? Did you mention him at all?"

"Kabiru? No… I… didn't – you think he's behind this?"

"I don't know… I'm just, worried."

"Attacking a church? What is Kabiru thinking? – I mean… if he's the one," Ijeoma stutters

"It's a little strange to me too. It might just be related to something else but… I'm just worried. If anything happened to John, I would… I could die," Aisha lets out.

"Don't say that, nothing will happen to him – hold on, let me turn on the TV."

*****

The morning Mass held at the Church of Assumption, Ikoyi, was quite solemn. Faithfuls were shocked to learn about the violent incident at their church, the night before.

John had made it to the church in time for the eight-a.m., Saturday morning Mass. The Parish Priest was assisted by deacon Benedict, who carried and read from the Book of the Gospels.

After the Communion had ended and the final prayer had been said, Father Aderemi had, during announcements, informed the Faithfuls about the horrific events of the previous night. A few of them who got to church early had already heard, from chatting with a few deacons.

Father Aderemi requested to see John in the Parish Office, after dismissing the people. John had gotten to speak to a few deacons who were at the rectory when the attack took place and he had gotten quite a lot of details.

He makes his way through the corridor of the Parish Office, to see Father Aderemi, feeling a heavy burden on his shoulders; he feels responsible for the events of last night.

"Good morning, Deacon Feyi," John greets the deacon seated outside the Parish Priest's office.

"Good morning, Father John," Feyi replies, with a somber look. "Father Aderemi is waiting for you."

"Thank you," John says, taking a step forward, knocking gently and then opening the door leading to the Parish Priest's office.

"Good morning, Father Aderemi," he says as he steps into the office and shuts the door.

"Good morning, Father John," Father Aderemi replies, unable to smile cordially, seated behind his desk, dressed in his white Cassock and hanging a large golden cross from his neck, "please sit."

"Thank you," John says humbly.

He takes his time and then says; "after your meeting with our Archbishop, I learned that the lady you have been romantically involved with, the same one you are planning to abandon your clerical duties for, is the daughter of the Emir of Kano," Father Aderemi charges, "I found it spurious that you will keep such a delicate part of the story from me because we discussed your relationship with Miss Aisha extensively, and all you told me, in that regard, was that she was a Muslim."

"I... am very sorry, Father," John responds, penitently, "I was wrong to have omitted it at the time."

"You do know that you have a responsibility to the church, first, as long as your Laicization has not been approved by His Holiness... and endangering the lives of your fellow members of Clergy, for whatever reason, shows complete nonchalance," he goes on, "it's apparent, without much scrutiny, that this whole fiasco is directly related to your involvements with Miss Aisha Mustapha. So, I need you to explain to me; exactly why did those armed men come here looking for you?"

John takes a moment to think but he still has no idea why he was being sought. "I... don't know yet, Father. There haven't been any factors within our relationship that could have led to such. I really can't be sure that this is directly related to my relationship with her," John lays out.

"I am quite confident, that it's all related to her. I was there to hear the things the assailants say," Father Aderemi imposes, disallowing John to disagree, "does her father, the Emir of Kano, approve of your relationship with her? With a Catholic? With a Catholic Priest?"

"We... are yet to get his approval but her mother has consented and promised to help make him understand."

"So, there you have the answer to the equation; her father doesn't like you and he wants to get rid of you. He is willing, and certainly has the power, to send a group of trained, armed men... now that he knows you're involved with his daughter."

"I... was with her last night and we went over possibilities; her father is a man of peace. He wouldn't —

"And yet you claim you have kept your Vow of Celibacy, Father John?"

"Yes, I have Father. I have told her we must wait, and we have both agreed to wait until we are married. It's not carnal desires that drive us together, Father, I can assure you; it is love."

The Parish Priest takes a deep breath, letting go of his pent-up aggression. "I did thank God last night, and I still did this morning, that you were not here for those men to apprehend..." Father Aderemi says, lovingly, "we would have lost a gentle soul – heaven knows what they would have done to you... we are in fellowship with the Savior and it is only glory to God, when we undergo persecutions like He did; men using evil to enforce their wishes. Still, we stand together and we will protect our own, and we will protect our faith... in your best interest, you should stay away from the rectory and even the church premises, until the police have solved this case. The Chief Inspector is on his way here, to ask you questions that might help us in apprehending these men, and hopefully, discover if the Emir of Kano is behind this. We could put you in a guest house for a few weeks."

"There will be no need for that, Father... I could move back to my Uncle's place, at the University of Lagos; it's quiet. I wouldn't want to burden the church financially, especially after last night's... discomfort. There will also be bills to pay for Richard who's in the hospital."

Father Aderemi keeps silent for a few moments, while saying a prayer for Richard, their Gateman and brother-in-Christ, remembering the horror he went through last night; bleeding out for almost an hour after being shot. "Even though we walk through the valley of the shadow of darkness, we shall fear no evil... for the Lord is with us," he declares, from his spirit.

"Amen," John replies.

"You should probably go and see Richard at the Gold Cross Hospital... but not before Chief Inspector Adebanjo gets here." He places both hands on the table and then curls his lips into a smile, "that will be all, for now."

"Okay, Father," John says, preparing to stand up, "peace be with you."

"Peace be with you," he replies. John walks out of the modestly furnished office. He opens the door and steps out, joining deacon Feyi. He finds deacon Benedict also, seated outside the office. John hadn't had the chance to talk with him, since he got to the church this morning.

"Good morning, Father John," Benedict says, getting up, as John shuts the door.

"Good morning, Deacon Benedict," John replies, keen to communicate with him.

"Can I speak with you privately?" Benedict asks, looking uneasy.

"Of course – sure."

They both walk down the hallway, towards John's office.

"I was able to have a look at the assailants before they put their scarves over their faces. I had just stepped out of the compound when I saw them walk in," Benedict begins to relay, as they walk down the hallway slowly, "one of the men looked familiar and I knew I had seen him before."

John gets to his office and opens the door, with his interest piqued by Benedicts direction. He enters.

"I had been searching my mind since last night, trying to remember where I had seen the man," Benedicts says, walking into the office behind John and shutting the door.

"And have you been able to remember?" John asks, eager for some revelation. He sits on the edge of his table and offers Benedict his full attention.

"I had to pray to God for remembrance and finally, I was taken to the exact point I saw him first... at the Buy-Right supermarket. I have also seen him a second time, here in the church; during the Bazaar, he came to buy our barbecue chicken –

"Who are you talking about?"

"Miss Aisha Mustapha's driver."

"What? But... I was with her last night and her driver was driving us around."

"I am not sure what his job is but there were two men with her at the supermarket, and I saw both men at the Bazaar too."

"Yes..." John recalls, "there was only one of them with us last night and she usually has two people with her..." John fades into his thoughts. Undeniably, this was all connected to Aisha. He feels the weight of guilt on his shoulders again; he was the one who gave into her; his weakness brought this chaos.

"I want to tell Father Aderemi as soon as possible but I wanted to let you know first."

"Thank you, Deacon Benedict. You should... tell him right away."

"You're welcome, Father," Benedict says, still lingering, "...could this mean that her family is behind the attack? – I learnt her father is Alhaji Aliu Mustapha; the Emir of Kano."

John pauses for a moment before replying. "It certainly seems so... even though I am sure, she knows nothing about it."

"I might still be wrong; I might be identifying the wrong person because I only caught a glimpse of his face, and it was dark. Maybe... you could get her to send you a picture of her drivers, so I could confirm? – before taking this to Father Aderemi."

John hums, considering the best approach to discover the truth. He pulls out his mobile phone from the pocket of his black trousers. "I'll just invite her over to the church."

*****

There is a knock on the door. Major Hassan isn't expecting anyone, still dressed his boxers and singlet, underneath his silk bathrobe, at one p.m. in the afternoon. He takes a sip out of the glass of brandy in his hand, before dropping it on the stool, and standing lazily off the living room sofa. He pauses the action movie he was watching.

"Who's there?" he blares, threateningly.

"Rasheed."

Hassan goes over and opens the door. "No work today?"

Rasheed enters, holding a newspaper. "Just coming from the office... it's a Saturday, so not much to do."

Hassan shuts the door and then walks past him, back towards the living room. He picks his glass and sits, before noticing that Rasheed is staring at him strangely. "What?" he barks.

Rasheed remains standing. "What have you done, Hassan?"

Hassan turns his attention back to the TV, uninterested in answering his question. "Get to the point," he drops.

"How can you attack a church, in Lagos?"

"What are you talking about?"

"This!" Rasheed unfolds the newspaper in his hand and pokes the front page while showing it to him.

"So, you think I'm behind that?"

"Of course, you are," Rasheed asserts, "the men went to the church looking for Father John – the same John I saw Aisha with – this is his picture," Rasheed stresses, poking the picture of John, inserted on the front page of the newspaper, "so, who else had a feud with him?"

"You never know," Hassan jibes, "these Christian pastors are fond of going around bedding other people's women. I'm just glad someone is after him. I almost wish I was the one."

Rasheed laughs, mockingly. "So, you think you sound convincing, right now? I am not fooled by you… I know what you're capable of. I am a firsthand witness to your madness. It's your gang of criminals you sent to do this job, right, or did you go yourself?"

"Don't speak stupidly of things you don't know about," Hassan, warns him, infuriated.

"I don't know? Me, who was there the night you all beat that man to death!"

"Keep your mouth shut!" Hassan growls, casting a hostile look at him.

"Look, Hassan," Rasheed says, lowering his voice and finally taking a seat, "this thing you have done is worse than what you did that night. This thing... is on the front page of the newspapers; it's on the TV."

"I had nothing to do with it!"

"This thing affects every Muslim and Christian," Rasheed continues, unconvinced by Hassan's denial, "in the country and all over the world. You just put some major heat on yourself – not to mention, this is a disgrace to Allah and to Islam. Are you going to justify your actions as noble? You acted out of jealousy."

"Dude, stop pissing me off. I said I had nothing to do with the attack on the church!"

"Look, I don't want to see you ruin your life because of Aisha. She is not yet your bride yet and since you find her unfaithful, leave her alone and give your attention to someone who deserves it. You can get almost any woman; it's not by force to marry the Emir of Kano's daughter."

"Who cares about her father being an Emir? I love her; I have loved Aisha since the first day she was betrothed to me and she was betrothed to me before her father became the Sultan of Kano. I'm not letting her go."

"So why don't you just do the proper thing; sit her down and ask her to leave this John guy. If she is still marriage-worthy, then she will apologize and do as you say... rather than taking insane actions."

Hassan pauses for a moment, thinking. He takes the last sip of Brandy from his glass. "Who the hell is John and what gives him the right to interfere with my relationship? I hope they catch him and kill him – be he a Priest or a Pope."

"Who are the 'they'? Your people, right?"

Hassan ignores him and gets up from the sofa. He heads towards his minibar, to pour himself another drink. Rasheed stands up also.

"You can deny it all you want but... my advice to you is; this is not the way forward. This is gives a bad name to every Muslim, like myself, and no one is going to take your side, if it is discovered that you're involved. I personally, am washing my hands off anything that involves this Pastor John and Aisha. I already regret telling you what I saw at the Oriental Hotel. If I knew this was what it would lead to, I would have kept it to myself." He throws the newspaper on the central table and heads out of the 1004 apartment.

"You want a drink?" Hassan asks, filling his glass up with brandy.

"No, thanks," Rasheed responds. He opens the front door and leaves.

"Suit yourself," Hassan says to the air before taking a sip.

*****

The black Mercedes S class pulls into the Church of Assumption compound, in Ikoyi. Aisha would usually have left her office at two p.m. on a Saturday but because of the unexpected call from John, she had to work faster and finish all she had to do before one p.m.

He didn't want to give her any details about why she was needed at the church, he simply made it clear to her that it was urgent. She could immediately construe that it was connected to the most prominent issue at the moment; the attack last night.

Nuru parks the car close to the church building. John is standing at the top of the stairs, along with one other man, both dressed in black. John is wearing his black trousers, a black button-up shirt and his white dog-collar. He presses his lips into a smile as Aisha opens her door to step down but he does not come to join her.

Aisha steps out of the black car, clutching her handbag, wearing a sparkling white Abaya and a red Hijab. She walks modestly and graciously towards the short flight of stairs, leading towards the church main entrance. She keeps her eyes on her feet as she climbs the stairs but looks up when she gets to the top.

"Hi," John says, stretching his palm out towards her.

"Hi," she replies, collecting his palm.

"Do you remember Deacon Benedict?"

"Yes," she says, smiling at Benedict, who's standing beside John, "I knew he looked familiar."

"Good afternoon, Miss Aisha," Benedict curtsies.

"Good evening," she replies.

"So..." Aisha breathes out, considering John's eyes, "I'm here. Why did you ask me to come?"

"Yes... we fear... your family might be, somehow, connected to the attack," John says.

"Oh – okay," Aisha swallows, "why do you think so?"

John takes a look at Benedict and then back at Aisha. "Benedict here, got to see the faces of one of the assailants and he believes he is your guard – I noticed he wasn't with us last night also."

"Yes..." Aisha says, "I haven't seen Abu since last night but I don't see how..." Aisha voice fades, as she is struck with a revelation. Still she knows she can't share her thoughts out loud now. She decides to keep it to herself.

"Do you have a picture of him, so I could confirm?" Benedict asks her. "I'm not a hundred percent sure, it was quite dark."

"Yes," Aisha says, "we took some pictures together at the Nikah – Abu and Nuru." She pulls out her phone from her bag and scrolls through. Aisha is finding it hard to look towards John. She feels a surge of shame wash over her; it is as though she is from a tribe of barbarians; as though she is one too. "This is him," she says, turning the phone screen towards Benedict.

"Yes! Yes, that's him," Benedict confirms, with his eyes popping open at the picture.

"Wow, I see..." Aisha says, pulling her phone back and staring at the picture, distant. She finally takes her eyes off the phone and takes a cautious look at John, through the corner of her right eye.

"Do you know where he is? Or where we can find him?" John asks, softly, "...the police would need to know."

"I would do my best to find him, and my driver, Nuru, would also help," Aisha states, fighting back her shame with a firm tone.

"The police would need to speak to you... just to get a clear idea of who he is and how well you know him – they're in the church office, waiting."

"Okay, that's fine," she responds.

"They would like to speak to your driver too – you say his name is Nuru?" Benedict adds.

"Yes. Sure," she spouts. She then turns towards the car and waves at the tinted windscreen. Nuru quickly opens the door and pops his head out.

"Yes, ma?!" Nuru inquires.

"Please lock the car and come," Aisha tells him. She then turns to John, just to consider his eyes and confirm if he still saw her the same way; to confirm if they were still undeniably on the same side. Through him, she sees her past and her future; she feels at peace; she knows he won't let anything tear them apart now.

*****

There are six empty glass bottles of fruity alcoholic cocktail on Ijeoma's kitchen counter. She got back to her private apartment in Ajah an hour ago, at three p.m., after working at her office on a Saturday, and decided to cook; cooking is her own form of therapy.

She boiled chopped pieces of chicken and she went ahead to fry them. She used the chicken broth to make a spicy curry sauce, then soaked the fried chicken pieces in it. She peeled a few Irish potatoes and boiled them. Now, she is mashing the potatoes.

A few tears ended up dropping from her eyes and mixing with the cooking, and now into the mashed potatoes. She has been crying and she wanted to spice her food with these tears.

After the phone call with Aisha this morning, she promised herself she would move forward and not look back anymore. Kabiru has trodden on her heart several times but this would be the last time. He broke her trust this time and proved to her that he is just an animal.

She serves herself a moderate plate of the mashed potatoes and the chicken curry sauce. She sets her cutlery and a bottle of water on a tray, along with her plate of food. She then walks over to her air-conditioned living room to place it on the stool beside her red, leather sofa. She switches on the flat screen TV with the remote control, turns down the volume and picks up her phone from the central table.

She scrolls through her phone as she walks back to the kitchen, floating on a cloud of tipsiness. She opens her kitchen fridge, pulls out her seventh bottle of fruity alcoholic cocktail and opens it. She then dials Kabiru's number, places the phone to her ear and takes the first sip of her new drink, while walking slowly back to the living room. Her therapy is done and now she has the strength to confront him. He picks up her call.

"Hi, baby," Kabiru chimes, over the phone.

"I'm guessing your fiancé is not around you; that's why you can say that out loud," she taunts, speaking in slow motion.

"No, she isn't. How are you?"

"I'll be better, after this phone call…" Ijeoma says, before taking a second sip of her drink. She continues walking slowly, past the living room and towards her bedroom, holding her drink in one hand and her phone to her ear, with the other hand. "Our relationship has… come to an end," she says, breathing out.

"You sound tipsy; what have you been drinking and what are you talking about?" he questions her, scoldingly.

"You…" she says, scoffing, "are a liar, a cheat, a dog, a fool, a beast. I wish – I wish I never met you; I wish I never fell in love with you…" she then slips into tears, "I allowed a devil into my heart."

"Can you get to the part where you tell me what you're talking about?" he asks, insensitively.

"Because of you… I never let any guy into my heart. I couldn't even see anyone else. I fell for you… and you watched me fall and break into pieces. I've been content being your secret girlfriend for so long; anything just to be with you… but what do I get? Betrayal, lies… neglect."

"This is a just tantrum you're throwing, Ijeoma, but I'll play along," he concedes, "I am sorry for not being around as much as I used to but how did I betray you and when did I lie to you?"

"Don't you dare play dumb; it's on the news! So, this is the real you? A thug; a criminal?" she accuses him, stepping into her bedroom. She drops the glass bottle on her dressing table.

"What? The attack on the Lagos church? I haven't really seen the details of –"

"Oh, shut up! The men went there looking for Father John – the same church I mentioned to you – you're lucky I'm not calling the police on you," she sneers.

"Went there looking for John? Is that what the news says?" he asks, stunned.

"I wasn't expecting the truth from you, anyway. I just called to let you know our relationship has come to an end – goodbye."

"Listen, Ijeoma, I had nothing –"

"I'm done listening to you, Kabiru! I'm done… I'm done with you… you've made me something I'm not. I'm not a liar, I don't betray my friends and I certainly don't help criminals gather information – I don't want to become like you; I don't want anything to do with you; I'm done with you," she gushes out before cutting the call.

She lowers the phone from her ear, slowly. A tear rolls down her face.

Her phone begins to vibrate. She looks at the screen and sees it's Kabiru calling. She throws the ringing phone on her bed and heads out of the bedroom.

She walks into the living room, sits on the sofa, picks up her plate of mashed potatoes and stares blankly at the TV, while more tears come down her face.

Kabiru was everything to her but she always knew she would never be with him. He never took her seriously enough; certainly not as seriously as Aisha took John. She always prayed for a love like theirs; a love that lasted this long and remained strong. Now she realizes she could never have that with Kabiru; he is the same person that ruined Aisha's love the first time and here he is again, ready to destroy it permanently.

There will be no looking back. This is the last time she would give her heart out so cheaply. All she wanted was for him to give his love to her but her own love wasn't enough to earn it.

She picks up her fork, carves out a chunk of mashed potatoes and dips it into the chicken curry sauce. She takes a breath and then puts her fork to her mouth.

CHAPTER 12

Karida makes her way up the stairs, followed by her maid, who is carrying a bed-tray with her husband's dinner. Like most days, since Alhaji (Dr.) Aliu Mustapha started residing at the Gidan Rumfa, she gets to spend the night with him.

She is the fifth wife, out of eight wives competing for his attention, but she has gained the superiority of a first wife, mostly because of her influence in securing Aliu's ascension to the throne, through the backing of the King of Saudi Arabia. Karida and her maid climb onto the third floor of the Emir's private quarters and walk down the carpeted hallway, towards his bedroom.

In the five years it took, between the time when Aliu was named as successor and the time when he became the new Sultan of Kano, Karida had become his pillar of support. He relied heavily on her for political and spiritual guidance. The late Emir remained sick all that while but refused to give up the ghost so easily, and the more time it took, the more the opposition gathered against Aliu's claim. In the end, it was Karida's powerful family influence that paved the way for him.

A guard stationed at the Sultan's door, steps aside for Karida to pass. She knocks on the door of Aliu's room and then opens it gently. She steps in, while her maid waits outside.

Alhaji Aliu Mustapha is seated on his king size bed, leaning on the cushioned headboard, with the TV in front of him turned on. He has taken off his royal attire, after meeting with the Governor of Kano and other officials this afternoon, in the Soron Ingilia; the English Hall, and is dressed in his grey Kaftan. He turns his face towards Karida, giving her his attention.

"Your dinner is ready, my love," she says.

"Okay, thank you," he says, before turning his attention back to the television.

Karida opens the room door again and calls on her maid; "bring it."

"Yes ma," the maid replies. She steps forward and hands the bed-tray to her madam. Karida collects the tray and heads back into the room while the maid shuts the door.

She walks across the room holding the tray, which has two plates covered in transparent film, a glass cup, a bottle of water and two sets of cutleries. She then places it beside him, before climbing onto the bed herself.

She peels the film off the plate of Jollof rice and the plate of fried goat meat in chili sauce. Aliu leans towards the tray, picks up his spoon, dips it into the Jollof rice and serves himself a taste. He chews through the rice, feeling the texture and assessing the taste.

"You like it?" Karida asks, knowing how choosy her husband gets.

"It's perfect," he replies. She smiles, content. "Join me," he says picking up the bed tray and placing it over his lap.

"I'll have a little," she obliges. Karida gets under the quilt, close beside him, and leans her back on the headrest. She then picks up the second set of cutleries. She scoops up a bit of the Jollof rice and then slides it through the chili sauce in the second plate, before putting it into her mouth.

Aliu is a slender and supple man, in his mid-sixties. He has never been the type to exert himself physically, even when younger, though he is not known to have had any health issues. He spends most of his days indoors, when not at an office, in prayer and silent meditation. His words are always carefully chosen, to avoid having unnecessarily long conversations with others.

Having been married to him for thirty-four years, since she was twenty-one years old, Karida has learned that Aliu prefers the company of people who know how to be quiet. She only brings up pressing matters for discussion and most times they just enjoy each other's company, without words.

Aliu believes that so much can be said without making a sound and appreciates Karida, above his other wives, for understanding that. It's partly why he prefers to spend most nights with her, apart from her superior understanding of how he likes his food. He keeps his attention on the TV, watching the International News on cable.

"There's a little problem we need to attend to," Karida says, requesting his attention, before setting his glass upright and filling it with drinking water.

He turns his face to her inquisitively, while still scooping some of the chili sauce and dropping it over the Jollof rice.

"...it's about Aisha... and her new boyfriend."

"Boyfriend? Is that what we're calling him now? You called me from Lagos and told me she wants to marry the catholic, young man, and I told you I can't support that."

"I know better than to argue with you but I'm hoping that in time you will change your mind," Karida pushes, "but there is an even more urgent issue at hand – the attack on the church in Lagos... is now directly related to us and to this catholic, young man; John – I told you he's a Pastor too."

Aliu drops his cutlery, sensing the seriousness of the conversation. He takes a gulp of water to wash the food down.

"Some people went to the church looking to attack Pastor John and it seems it was because they knew he had been spending time with our daughter..." Karida pauses, to allow Aliu absorb the first bit of information, "the police have started investigating and, as it turns out, one of the attackers has been identified as Abu; a member of our staff; one of Aisha's personal guards. So, now the police have reasons to believe that our family was involved in the attack on the church... I spoke with Aisha on the phone and she told me that she's spoken with the police this afternoon and promised them to help catch Abu... but until they catch him, the rumor is that 'our family disapproved of the union and tried to eliminate pastor John'."

Aliu takes a few seconds to piece through the information he just received. "So... what's the real story?" he asks her.

"Aisha believes that Hassan Ibrahim is behind the attack. That's what she told me on the phone. She remembers one time where he called Abu and asked him to take her car home and Abu did so without even confirming with her. It makes sense, if he found out that she was in love with John through the guard, he would have known exactly where Aisha had been going to meet him. Not to mention, General Ibrahim was the one who gave us most of our security personnel.

"Yes, he did," Aliu agrees, "but I'm forced to believe that Hassan did this without his father's knowledge, if indeed he is the one behind it." Aliu picks up his fork and knife, while still thinking on all he has heard, and cuts a piece of fried goat meat into two. He pokes one and lifts it into his mouth. Karida also takes some time to think, in his presence.

"It could be on the news tomorrow. How do we keep this from getting out of hand?" she asks, worried.

Aliu finishes chewing the meat and takes another gulp of water. "We can't bring the Ibrahims into this, until we are sure Hassan is involved. You and your daughter are the ones who allowed things to get out of hand, in the first place," he scolds, "we'll just have to weather the storm ourselves for now, until Abu is found. In the meantime, get Kabiru on the phone; I want to find out what he knows or thinks of this; he and Hassan are friends." Aliu picks up his phone from the bedside cabinet and hands it to Karida.

"Okay." She dials Kabiru's number and puts the phone on speaker, while holding it up.

"Hello, daddy," Kabiru greets, over the phone.

"Kabiru," his mother speaks.

"Yes, mommy."

"We have a pressing family issue. Your father needs to ask you some questions and we need the truth," she announces.

"Kabiru," Aliu starts.

"Yes, daddy."

"I hear that Hassan might have been involved in the attack on the Lagos church; is this true?"

"I... don't know for sure, daddy, but it is very possible," Kabiru replies.

"What do you know?" Aliu asks, firmly.

"When I was in Lagos... Hassan found out that Aisha was seeing someone else and he got very angry. He decided he wanted to find the John and teach him a lesson but... as far as I know, he hadn't yet discovered where to find him before I left Lagos. It's possible he might have found out on his own, daddy."

"So, you were involved in planning an attack on the Pastor, in a Church?" his father asks, astounded.

"No, daddy! We didn't even know he was a Pastor at the time – and I thought Hassan was just going to bully him a little, I didn't think he would send armed men."

"Who else knew about this?"

"Just Hassan, myself and Rasheed Aregbesola... but I doubt Rasheed could have been involved."

"Come and see me in the morning, you need a slap on the face – that is what you get for acting like a foolish revolutionist. How dare you place Hassan's wishes over your own sister's; your own family's?"

Kabiru has nothing to say in response. He remains quiet over the phone. Aliu shoves Karida's hand away, which is holding the phone close to his mouth, grunting. He then picks up his cutlery and attempts to returns to his food.

"Goodnight, Kabiru. See you in the morning," Karida says into the phone, while considering the look of displeasure on her husband's face, and getting ready to receive her own share of scolding.

"Goodnight, mommy," Kabiru replies. She cuts the call.

"What kind of embarrassment is this?!" he yells at her, dropping his cutlery loudly on the ceramic plate, "you need to keep your children in order! This liberty you've given them is too much! Too much. This is a large family. There are a lot of people to consider."

"I'm sorry, my love. Please forgive me."

*****

"The Pastor was doing the do-do with Miss Aisha Mustapha and that is what caused her family to retaliate – it is as clear as day!" Kunle Adepoju, the Morning Catch-Up co-host, blares over the television in Hassan's living room. Nkechi Ejiofor; the host and Kemi Adigun; the second co-host, both laugh.

"Kunle, please!" Nkechi exclaims, swallowing her laughter. Kemi also forces herself to stop laughing.

"Let us stay away from assumptions. I know Catholic Priests take a vow of celibacy and Father John has not said to have broken his," Kemi Adigun, the calm, beautiful and articulate TV co-host, contributes.

"Because they used to stamp it on the fore-head, abi?" Kunle jeers. The two ladies let out muffled laughs.

"If he had," Kemi continues, fighting her laughter, "the Clergy would have known."

"Because they used to put alarm down there, abi?" he furthers. Kemi and Nkechi burst into an unintended laughter.

"That's enough, Kunle, we hear you," Nkechi regains control of the show, "in case you're just joining us, this is the Sunday Morning Catch-up show, and we have been discussing the front-page story on all major newspapers this morning," Nkechi says, picking up a newspaper from the table in front of her and displaying it to viewers. Abu's picture is enlarged on the front page, with the headline 'WANTED'. "Abu Hussein, has been identified as one of the attackers of the Catholic church in Ikoyi, the day before yesterday," Nkechi narrates, "as it turns out, he is under employment by the Emir of Kano, Alhaji Aliu Mustapha, being one of his daughter's body guards. Now, the plot gets even thicker; Father John, who these assailants went to the church looking for, is 'romantically involved' with the Emir's daughter, Miss

Aisha Mustapha, the same person Abu Hussein was employed to guard. This begs the question –"

There is a gentle knock on the front door. Hassan quickly lowers the volume of the TV and then switches it off, knowing who it might be. He gets up from his sofa and walks towards the door, fully dressed, in laced black leather shoes, blue jeans, a tucked in blue, short-sleeve button-up shirt, a black leather belt and a black, leather-strapped watch.

He opens the door and sees Aisha, as he expected. She had called him last night to remind him of their usual Sunday meet-up. He hadn't heard from her in over a week, and in that time so much has changed.

"Hi, Hassan," Aisha says, with her usual innocent smile.

"Hi," he replies, stepping aside for her to come in. He notices her driver, Nuru, standing by on the corridor balcony, behind her. "Why is he here?" Hassan asks her, of Nuru.

"He's going to wait here for me; I won't be staying long," she replies, as she steps in, dressed in a red, long-sleeve dress, tied around the waist with a white fabric belt, mounting a red Hijab and clutching her white handbag in her right hand.

Hassan gives an unfriendly look to Nuru before shutting the door behind her. 'Why should Aisha's guard have to escort her to his door?' he thinks. "How are you?" he asks her, following her into his living room.

Aisha walks tentatively, frightened of her environment; frightened of the person behind her. She places her handbag on the single sofa and then takes a seat. He takes a seat on the long sofa, beside her. "I'm... okay," she replies, after taking her time, "I... came here today, so we could see each other face-to-face – I should have... done this earlier but things happened really, really fast," she explains.

"What things?" he asks, acting aloof.

"I'm sure you're well-aware... it's on the news this morning. I knew it was going to get out and that's why I had called you last night, to schedule this meeting."

"So... go ahead. I'm here, face-to-face," he says, leaning back into his chair.

"I... can't marry you, Hassan, and I'm really sorry for wasting your time. I hope... one day you would be able to forgive me. I fell in love with John... back when I was eighteen, but I had to let him go because of my dad becoming Emir. Now, we reconnected and I realized I'm still in love with him..."

"So... that's why you wouldn't give me your heart all this time... why you wouldn't let the world know that you were mine... because you always loved John... what's so special about him?" he asks, inconsolably.

"I… I just feel happier and loved, with him…"

"I don't make you feel loved?!"

"No, Hassan… you make me feel afraid," she says sincerely, knowing it might hurt.

He looks her deep in the eyes, protesting, but sees that she is truly frightened. He turns his face away from her and then stands off the long sofa. He walks over to his minibar and pulls out his pack of cigarettes. He opens the pack and pulls out a stick, along with his lighter. "How do I make you feel afraid?" he asks, before lighting his cigarette.

"You… take things too far, Hassan… you like dangerous things… you're violent –"

"I'm a soldier! I'm a Major in the Nigerian army!" he argues.

"But you don't know how to separate your work on the field from your life at home. You drive like you're in a warzone – look, the truth is simply that, I want to be happy… and only John can do that, so please… don't take him away from me. I know Abu must have told you things that you weren't supposed to know and he definitely gave you the wrong impression but… kidnapping him or harming him, or even killing him, is not going to stop my love for him. If you care about me, then let me be happy."

"So… you think I'm the one who planned the attack on him?" he asks her, after blowing out smoke.

Aisha takes a few breaths before continuing. "Abu is going to be found sooner or later but before he is, I'm hoping we can settle our differences and find a way to make this all disappear. I know I offended you but breaking the law is not a solution. I spoke to my dad this morning and he knows you might be involved. He's willing to protect you because of his relationship with your father... but *we* need to settle our differences now."

"I had nothing to do with the attack. Don't just come here throwing accusations!" he barks at her.

"Okay," she backs off, "let's just wait until Abu is found." She gets up from the sofa and picks her handbag

"You think I'm the only one who has been offended by Pastor John; look closer and you'll find that you're not the only woman he is bedding; I'm not the only one who might wish him harm," Hassan ridicules.

Aisha takes a stern look at him. "Yes, we might have slept in the same bed but we have never had sex; I am still a virgin and if I decide to give my virginity to him, I know I'll be giving it to someone who loves me; someone I can trust." She turns towards the door and heads out.

"We're not done, here, Aisha!" he yells at her. She stops and turns her face to him. "I have spent ten years in this relationship and I'm not letting go!"

"I can never marry you, Hassan," she says softly. She continues towards the door.

"Don't you dare walk out! You are betrothed to me!" He approaches her.

"I'm not your property Hassan... not yet. Not ever." She opens the front door. Nuru is standing by, waiting. "Let's go," she says to him. Hassan gets to the door, just as Aisha steps onto the seventh-floor corridor balcony of the 1004 Apartments building. She immediately feels safer as she walks away from his front door and towards the elevator. Nuru walks behind her. It's some minutes to nine, in the morning, but the sun isn't shining yet because of the heavy rain in the earlier hours of the morning.

Hassan stands at his door, watching them leave, with a resentful look on his face. He feels as though his reason for living is leaving him. He won't grovel, he won't argue but he decides he won't take defeat.

*****

Felix Nneji, the Pastor of the Second Coming Pentecostal Church and the founder of C.U.A.V, Nigeria; the Christian Union Against Violence, Nigeria, is backed by over fifty people, and they're hoisting up their placards, chanting 'STOP THE VIOLENCE!', 'WE WON'T TAKE IT ANYMORE!', standing in front of the Mustapha's Lekki residence. He had rallied thirty-two people to join him in protesting, during his Sunday morning sermon, at his church. He also got the participation of about twenty area boys and vagabonds, who were willing to cause a little trouble for a few thousand Naira.

He faces the mob of young men and women who have joined him in staging this demonstration, and raises up his hands, motioning them to listen to his speech.

"Many of us here have been victims of religious violence or at least we have family and friends who have been victims!" Pastor Felix, an energetic man in his early forties, shouts to his followers, reveling in the attention, "every time, we the Christians are the ones who get slaughtered by the Muslims! Why?! Because we act gentle and peaceful but they act violent and wicked! When last did Christians go about harming Muslims? But they do that to us regularly! When last did we go and attack a Mosque and the Imam inside? But they did that to us, just two days ago! In Lagos, here! ARE WE GOING TO STAND BACK AND DO NOTHING?"

"NO!!!" the crowd replies, vehemently.

"When I was just eighteen years old, living with my father and mother in Jos," he tells his story, inspiring attention, "we were attacked by Muslims in our home! Why?! Because we were 'infidels', they said! They killed my father and mother, in front of me! With cutlasses and sticks, like they were wild animals! And left me there to cry over them! ...while they went on killing other innocent victims," Pastor Felix narrates, overpoweringly, "back then, I could not do anything but I won't let it happen again! ARE WE GOING TO STAND BACK AND DO NOTHING?"

"NO!!!" the crowd proclaims.

"So, join me, in sending them a message," he says, picking up a pebble from the floor, "a message that they will understand. This is the Emir of Kano's house and it has been discovered that the Emir is the one hiring people to go and attack churches. They say because his daughter is in love with a Pastor, so he wants to kill the all the Pastors; they want to bring their violence down here, to Lagos too! All these wicked people are living inside this compound!" He points at the Mustapha's residence, standing just in front of the pavement leading to the gate, "so, we are going to do what the Muslims call 'Ramī Al-Jamarāt'; Stoning of the Devil. The Muslims do it when they go for their pilgrimage, in Mecca. Pick up a stone... go ahead, pick up any stone... and throw it at this their gate. The Devil is standing there, so stone him, until he disappears!" Pastor Felix goes ahead and swings the first stone, as hard as he can, at the high-rising black metal gate leading into the Emir's Lagos residence. It sends out a loud clank. He steps aside, allowing the other fifty-two people to throw their stones. "Throw it!" he commands. They swing them at the gate, sending a thunderous rush of threatening sounds to the inhabitants of the residence.

"That is one!" he instructs his hostile followers, "we are going to throw it seven times! ...because that is how they do it in Mecca. Seven times, until the Devil disappears!" Pastor Felix picks up his second stone from the ground.

*****

While driving Aisha into their compound, less than thirty minutes ago, Nuru had to drive through the large group of people that had gathered in front of the entrance, after he had horned severally and they finally stepped aside languidly. He was driving Aisha back to the house from the Lagos Oriental Hotel.

It's some minutes past five p.m. and the crowd of protesters has now switched from being a nuisance to being a menace. The loud clanks on the gate have alerted all the seven trained guards in the compound, the other six working for other members of the Mustapha's extended family. Nuru, who is in his late thirties, seems to be the most infuriated of the seven. He walks towards the black Mercedes S class parked within the compound, opens the driver's door and pulls out his black, Browning 1911-22 semi-automatic pistol, from beneath his seat. He then shuts the car door and heads towards the compound gate, while the other six guards simply observe.

Nuru graduated from the Nigerian Military Academy when he was twenty years old. Five years later, he got his first job as a personal guard for a rich businessman in Bauchi state. Six years after that, he got a job guarding one of the sons of the late Emir of Kano. After the passing away of the previous Emir, he started working for Alhaji Aliu Mustapha and he was given the responsibility of guarding his daughter. In his long career as a personal guard and driver, he has only had to violently defend his employers three times and on all three occasions he succeeded, killing the assailants and protecting the life of his employers.

He looks into the gatehouse, at the gateman. "Bello, and you're looking at these people doing this nonsense!"

"Oga, what I fit do?" he defends, displaying his empty palms.

"Come, open gate," Nuru says, cocking his pistol.

Bello quickly walks towards the gate, seeing through the gatehouse window that the protesters were about to pick a new set of stones. "Yes, sir." He opens the pedestrian gate for Nuru, using the metal gate as a shield in case stones are thrown. Nuru steps out.

The protesters, who were about to throw their third set of stones, halt as the pedestrian gate is opened. Nuru points his semi-automatic pistol towards the sky and lets off two loud shots. They all duck and rush backwards, away from him, except for Pastor Felix.

"The Devil has appeared!" Pastor Felix proclaims to his crowd, "these are the kind of people that go about killing Christians! These are the people that the Emir is hiring to attack churches! ARE WE GOING TO STAND BACK AND DO NOTHING?" he calls to his protesters.

A few of them answer. "NO!!!"

"ARE WE GOING TO STAND BACK AND DO NOTHING?!" he calls a second time, with venom.

"NO!!!" all members of the mob respond, defiantly, "'STOP THE VIOLENCE!', 'WE WON'T TAKE IT ANYMORE! 'STOP THE VIOLENCE!', 'WE WON'T TAKE IT ANYMORE!" they begin to chant, loudly.

"ALL OF YOU, GET OFF THIS PROPERTY, NOW!" Nuru yells back, at the top of his voice!

"We are not on your property, we are on the road!" Pastor Felix responds, causing the crowd to pause their chanting, "or do you own the road too?!"

"Allah, I will shoot all of you if you throw any stone at this gate again!"

"Oga Nuru," Bello calls, "Madam Aisha dey call you."

Nuru is upset but he must respond to his employer's call, just when he was sending his message to these nasty pests. "I dey come," he says to Bello. He then gives a threatening look to the Pastor before heading back into the compound through the pedestrian gate.

"The Devil has come to scare us! Will we be afraid?!" Pastor Felix Nneji incites his crowd.

"NO!!!" they shout back. Nuru ignores them and enters.

"Tell the Devil, like Jesus did; 'get thee behind me, Satan!' Pick up your stones and stone the Devil." Pastor Felix throws his third stone, which remained in his fist, at the large gate, just after the gateman shuts the pedestrian gate.

Aisha is standing beside her car, with the door to the owner's corner opened, looking at Nuru furiously as he approaches. "What are you doing?" she scolds him.

"Madam, they are causing trouble outside!" Nuru defends, getting to the driver's side of the car. Another thunderous sound can be heard, as the mob throws their third set of stones at the gate.

"And that's why you're shooting at them?" she asks Nuru, incredulously.

"I shot up, so that they can move back."

"Please, don't try that again. The whole family is already under heavy scrutiny from the public; the last thing we need right now is shooting at unarmed Christian protesters!" she corrects him, firmly, "get in the car and take me back to the hotel," she spits out, before sitting in the car and shutting her door.

"Yes, madam," Nuru says, opening his door. He conceals his gun under his seat before entering, shutting the door and starting the car. He horns at Bello, to open the gate, as he turns the car around.

Bello opens the gate, giving a clear view of the compound to the fifty-three-people gathered outside. He then hides behind the thick metal to avoid being hit by stones. Nuru drives out of the compound, horning furiously at crowd to make way.

They begin to hoist up their placards as they slowly give way, chanting 'STOP THE VIOLENCE!', 'WE WON'T TAKE IT ANYMORE!'. Aisha looks at the faces of the aggrieved people, through her tinted windows, wishing they could understand that she never meant anyone harm.

Nuru turns into the street and drives away from the compound. She picks up her phone, dials John and puts it to her ear. She had left the hotel just some minutes after four p.m., after he had not yet returned from the church. She understood that it was a Sunday and that he would have a lot to do, especially with the recent chaos.

She thought she would be able to spend some quiet time at home and maybe get Zainab; their longtime maid and cook, to whip her up a nice late-lunch, but the presence of protesters outside the compound made the house unbearable.

"Hello, dear," John says over the phone.

"Where are you?" she asks.

"I'm just on my way back to the hotel. How about you?"

"On my way to the hotel too; just leaving my house – it's really crazy; there are some Christian protesters outside our compound, really causing a fuss. They were throwing stones at the gate continuously; making so much noise," she complains.

"Wow! That's terrible. Hope they weren't damaging anything?"

"Not really, maybe denting the gate a bit, but then my driver went at them with a gun – I told him that was wrong – hold on, I have a call waiting." She pulls her phone from her ear to check the screen and sees it's Ijeoma calling. "It's Ijeoma calling, I'll call her back," she says to John, after putting the phone back to her ear.

"Which Ijeoma? Your friend from Unilag?"

"Yeah! You remember," she says, smiling.

"You two are still close?"

"Well, we just reconnected some days ago. She came to the Nikah I went for."

"Cool... I really need to spend some time with you, I'm just turning into the Hotel now. All these things going on... you're my source of peace."

"You're my peace too... I'm on my way, love."

"Okay."

"Okay, bye."

"Love you," John concludes. She cuts the call as Nuru turns into another street, leading away from the inner streets and towards the main road of Lekki Phase-one. She looks out her window, thinking about her father; how he must feel now that the whole nation wrongfully thinks he was behind the attack and how noble he is to say nothing in his defense.

She remembers she missed a call from Ijeoma. She decides to call back, just as Nuru slows down to climb a road bump.

The glass window of the driver's door is shattered, as two loud gun shots are heard. Aisha's face and clothes are sprayed with blood, splattering out of Nuru's impaled skull. She screams, horrorstruck. The car comes to a halt over the road bump, while still on, as Nuru slumps towards the front passenger seat, lifeless.

She notices two men approaching, on both sides of the vehicle, with their faces covered in black cloth; one with his long rifle pointed at the driver's door and another holding a pistol and heading towards the owner's corner, where she is seated. She jabs the door lock but notices that it's already locked. The man with the pistol smashes her window with the butt of his pistol and unlocks the door himself. Aisha ducks and covers her face to avoid the glass shards from harming her, while the second man with the rifle confirms that Nuru is incapacitated, pointing his rifle at him through the smashed driver's window.

The man with the pistol opens her door, removes a white handkerchief from his pocket and places it over her face, as he attempts to get her out of the vehicle.

Aisha screams, seeking the help of people nearby, but as she catches her breath to scream a second time, she inhales a strange odor through the handkerchief and falls into an overwhelming sleep.

CHAPTER 13

John hasn't been able to get any sleep for two nights. He has been praying repeatedly, for the Lord to bring back his love to him, alive.

He is alone in his office, at the Church of Assumption, Ikoyi, dressed in black pants, black shoes, black button-up shirt and his white clerical collar, with the TV turned on, watching the morning news. There have been various speculations about the abduction of the Emir's daughter but John feels, deep in his heart, that Hassan might be behind this. Aisha had told him about her suspicions, the last night they spent together at the Lagos Oriental; that the person she was betrothed to was behind the attack on his Church; behind the attempt to abduct him. She had explained that she was going to break it off with Hassan permanently on Sunday morning, while John was at the Mass.

"...the Saint Thomas Cathedral in Sabon Gari, Kano, was burnt down last night by Muslim religious extremists, accusing Christians for the abduction of the Emir's daughter," Nkechi Ejiofor, the authoritative TV host broadcasts, over the television in Father John's office, "Pastor Felix Nneji and five other members of Christian Union Against Violence, who were staging a riot in front of the Emir's Lagos residence, the same time Aisha Mustapha was abducted, have been arrested by the police in connection with the abduction. The police are still yet to determine if they had anything to do with the kidnapping of the Emir of Kano's daughter and the killing of her driver, Mr. Nuru Mohammed, but it was in reaction to this that the crowd of Muslim fanatics in Kano took to burning down the Saint Thomas Cathedral. Luckily, no life was claimed but the Cathedral was razed to the ground."

"If this goes on, Nkechi, we just might have a nationwide, religious crisis on our hands," Kemi Adigun, the co-host of the Morning Catch-Up show, warns, "people need to stop taking the law into their own hands; let the law enforcement agencies do their job. I don't think Pastor Felix Nneji and his people were behind the abduction but they certainly shouldn't have been throwing stones at the Emir's gate! How does that solve the problem, really?"

"As we know, the late Nuru Mohammed is said to have fired gun shots, outside the compound, at Pastor Felix and his crowd, to scare them away," Kunle Adepoju injects, "that might be the reason why they killed him and ended up abducting Miss Aisha Mustapha."

"So, you are concluding that Pastor Felix Nneji is behind the abduction?" Nkechi prods Kunle.

"I won't call it a conclusion; only an assumption, but it is certainly what the police and the public believe right now; that's why he was arrested and that's why some Muslims went ahead to burn a church last night, in Kano... who knows what will happen next?"

"Let's hope for the best and pray for peace," Nkechi says, moving the show forward, "also, in the news today; police still looking for Abu Hussein; the prime suspect in last week's attack on the Church of Assumption in Ikoyi, Lagos. If you have any information which can help in capturing him, please supply it to the nearest police station."

"We all know the Emir or members of his family were behind that attack on the Church of Assumption," Kunle spouts, carelessly, "his staff, Abu Hussein, is the main suspect and up until now, the Emir has not come out to deny the allegations against him."

"Yet another 'conclusion', Kunle," Nkechi warns.

"I'm only speaking my mind, Nkechi, based on what I see. I'm sorry I am not as good at mincing my words, like the pretty Kemi here."

"I think that the same people who carried out the attack on the Lagos church, Abu Hussein and his gang, are also responsible for the abduction of Miss Aisha. Abu *might* have been following the Emir's orders, or members of the Mustapha's large family, or he might be part of some religious, radicalistic sect but I doubt Pastor Felix and the C.U.A.V had anything to do with the abduction," Kemi drives her point home, disregarding Kunle's comments, "first, the abductors came fully armed; they executed a trained guard and successfully kidnapped Miss Aisha Mustapha, in a populated neighborhood, like Lekki Phase-one; they had to have been well-trained. Secondly, the

C.U.A.V were only armed with stones and noise, not guns and bullets – they are not trained militants and neither do they have a history of such levels of violence."

"So, you think the Emir could be behind the abduction of his own daughter?" Kunle asks her, fascinated.

"Yes, it is quite possible," Kemi responds, "let us not forget the relationship between the late Princess Diana and her late lover; Dodi Fayed; the son of the Egyptian billionaire; Mohamed Al-Fayed. Both families, the British royal family and the wealthy Al-Fayed family, were not happy about the two being in love. They sought many ways to separate them and in the end, Diana and Dodi both died in a mysterious car crash!" Nkechi and Kunle nod their heads, concurring with her, "it is quite clear, from what we know, that Miss Aisha Mustapha and Father John Amaechi are in love. The first attempt at abducting Father John was unsuccessful and maybe that's why they decided to take Miss Aisha out of the picture; maybe it's so much of an abomination for two lovers from strong, varying religious backgrounds to be together and, as we can see, they have succeeded in separating Aisha and John. This brings us back to my initial point; we have no idea what is going on; who is behind these attacks and what their motive is, so it is foolish of Nigerians to take the law into their own hands; to seek jungle-justice when they don't even know who committed the crime."

John's door is opened, distracting him from the television, and deacon Benedict pops his head in. "Miss

Ijeoma, is here to see you, Father. She says she is Miss Aisha Mustapha's close friend?"

"Ijeoma? Please, send her in," John replies, curious.

"Yes, Father." Benedict leaves and shuts the door.

John returns his attention to the heated Morning Catch-up show. "We have to take a commercial break but we'll be right back!" Nkechi Ejiofor inserts, "when we return, we're going to be discussing Pope Francis' open letter, made public early this morning and addressed to Nigerian Christians."

John's door is opened again and Ijeoma walks in, dressed in a fitted, purple skirt suit, with a white inner top and carrying a green handbag. He stands up and walks towards the door to greet her. "Hello... Father John," she says, forcing a joyful smile.

"Hello, Ijeoma," John replies, smiling warmly and stretching out his palm for a gentle handshake, "haven't seen you in years."

"Me neither." She collects his hand. "Thanks for seeing me."

"No problem at all; you're welcome anytime. Please have a seat," he says, before heading back to his chair and taking his seat opposite her. He can't figure out what she would want to talk about but he's sure it will be related to Aisha and hopefully, something that could help in finding her.

"How are you holding up, with Aisha missing?

"Oh… it's been torture… but I'm praying to God, to keep her safe and return her."

"By the worshipful intercession of Mary, He will answer favorably. Aisha is a good person, with a loving heart. She doesn't deserve any of this," Ijeoma consoles.

"She is God's daughter. I know He will keep her," John concludes. "What brings you here?" he then asks, eagerly.

"Yes, emmm… Aisha told me that you and she had gotten back together – at the Nikah, last week – and that you were now a Priest, at this Church so… I knew where to find you."

John listens attentively, as Ijeoma stutters, waiting for a glimmer of hope from the information she has come to offer.

"I tried calling her on Sunday evening but I wasn't able to reach her, and the next morning I heard the news that she had been abducted. I was calling her so… that I could confess to her… that I had betrayed her… that I lied to her… that I… sold her out. I thought I was doing it for love but now I realize that I was wrong."

"What do you mean?" he asks, befuddled.

"I'm going to make my Confession to you, here," Ijeoma continues, penitently, "…forgive me Father, for I have sinned… I had been in a relationship with Aisha's brother, Kabiru, for seven years now, and I never told her about it. I lied to her whenever the topic came up... I pretended, so she wouldn't notice... and worst of all... I made a deal with the Devil..."

"Continue..." he offers.

"I... am the reason why the men came to attack your church... I told Kabiru everything he needed to know, after Aisha had told it to me, at the Nikah; about what you do and where you stay... he, Hassan and Rasheed wanted to punish you for... stealing Aisha."

"Hassan? ...who is Rasheed?" John asks, ingesting what she came to say.

"Rasheed is their close friend. He was the one who saw you with Aisha, at the Oriental Hotel. They... asked me to spy on Aisha and find out about you, and I did... because Kabiru asked me... and I loved him and was willing to do anything for him but... I was wrong... Kabiru's a Devil."

"Kabiru? Aisha told me that she thought Hassan did this, with the help of her guard. She knew Abu and Hassan had been communicating. Plus, Kabiru had promised their father and mother that he was not involved in the attack on the church."

"So, you think Kabiru was not involved; that Hassan did it on his own?"

"Yes... I truly think Kabiru was not involved, not in the church attack and certainly not in her abduction. I suspect Hassan, alone, is behind both. He had the help of Abu, who was close enough to know every place Aisha goes, and Aisha had just broken it off with him in the morning, the same day she got kidnapped."

Ijeoma takes a few moments to consider John's point of view. Could it be that she was wrong to judge Kabiru?

"Do you know much about Hassan?" John asks her, racing down the route of his assumption, "where does he live? Could he be keeping her there?"

"I know him quite well... but Kabiru would know more. If you think Hassan might be behind her abduction – and I know he is crazy enough to plan such – then we should tell Kabiru. He would tell us what to do – I don't have to go to work today, so we can drive around town and search. Let me call him," Ijeoma says, reaching into her handbag for her phone, slightly happy that she was wrong about Kabiru; that she could trust him again; happy that it wasn't through her that the information was leaked. She dials his number.

John concurs with her decision, believing that he is one step closer to finding Aisha.

*****

Kabiru is almost through with his English breakfast, seated at the dining table with his mother, in their living quarters, within the Gidan Rumfa. He's had to be on his best behavior, ever since his father and mother discovered that he was cohorts with Hassan, in planning an attack on Pastor John.

With the recent abduction of Aisha, his mother has been thrown into a great depression. She, and everyone else in their family, believed that this was a retaliation by the Christians for the Muslim attack on the Catholic church, which involved Abu; their staff. The whole country and the world at large, believed that her husband was guilty of trying to abduct Father John, even though there was no clear evidence to indict the Emir.

Kabiru knows he is required to carry the blame, because he knew about Hassan's intentions, which have now turned into a nationwide conflict and resulted in the abduction of his sister. He called Hassan to drill him about the attack on the church but he denied it vehemently and now the whole family has to wait till Abu has been captured before they can undisputedly prove his innocence.

He watches Karida struggle to eat her breakfast, feeling penitent; her first meal since she heard the news that Aisha was taken. His phone, which is placed on the table beside his dining tablemat, vibrates. He looks towards it and sees it's Ijeoma calling. He quickly grabs the phone, stands up from the table and heads towards the kitchen in the next room.

"Let me get some more milk for my tea," he tells his mother, excusing himself. Karida looks toward him with her heavy eyes but does not speak. He gets into the kitchen and picks up the call. "Hello," he answers, heading outside, through the kitchen backdoor.

"Hi," Ijeoma returns, over the phone.

"I have been calling you for days and days. How could you just ignore me like that?! What is wrong —"

"Listen, Kabiru, I didn't call to fight. I just want to ask you this question and I need you to be honest."

"When last did I lie to you? Why would you doubt me?" He steps outside, not wanting to let his mother hear his conversation.

"Did you… tell Hassan what I told you at the Nikah, about John?"

"No, I did not! I was trying to tell you that but you wouldn't listen. You think I'm crazy enough to attack a church? You told me not to say anything and I did as you said!"

"Then… I'm really sorry, for doubting you… and for all the things I said. Please, forgive me. It was just so much of a coincidence."

Kabiru takes a breath. "I forgive you… and I miss you, terribly. Please don't ignore me like that again, it's too painful, especially now, with everything going on in my family."

"It was painful for me too, not being able to pick your calls... I'm at the church now, with John."

"John?"

"Yes. I came to see him, to discuss about Aisha. He was the one who convinced me that you were not involved... John believes that Hassan is behind Aisha's abduction. He said she had just broken up with Hassan on Sunday morning."

"Are you sure it wasn't done by the Christians? Would Hassan dare do such? Kidnap my sister?"

"If he could attack a church, I don't think this should be too farfetched."

"He denied attacking the church but I don't believe him. He certainly won't confess to kidnapping my sister... if he's behind this, he is going to pay heavily."

"What should we do? Go to his house and check?"

"No, don't. I don't want anything to happen to you and I doubt he would keep her there. Instead... call Rasheed and go see him. I spoke to him last week and he thought Hassan was behind the attack on the church too. Rasheed can help – tell him I asked him to – he knows a lot more about Hassan than I do. He just might know where Hassan would hide her."

"Okay, we'll call him."

"I'm going to tell my father about this; he needs to know Hassan might be behind Aisha's abduction."

"Okay."

"And I'll come to Lagos as soon as possible," he adds.

*****

The boiled yam and garden-egg sauce served to Alhaji Aliu Mustapha for breakfast, by his first wife; Alhaja Amina, isn't finding its way down his aged digestive system pleasurably. It's for reasons like these that he likes most of his meals prepared by Karida but, a few times a week, he allows his other wives do the cooking, to maintain peace between the eight he married.

He is not cautious in showing his displeasure with her food; he has not made it halfway through his meal in almost an hour, seated at the main dining room of the Emir's private quarters, with only Amina beside him. He loves his wife but he loves his stomach also, and only wishes to fill it with that which pleases him, seeing as he has worked hard enough to deserve it. He has been more focused on the newspaper in his hands, only stopping occasionally to taste the food again and confirm his repulsion for it, before washing it down the taste with cold water.

As usual, her husband, the Sultan of Kano, is quiet and cold during the little time that they spend together. He has a good excuse today because his 'prize-daughter' is missing and, in addition to that, the worldwide news has been smearing his name for the past few days, in connection with the attack on the Lagos church and with yesterday evening's burning of the Catholic church in Kano.

In her mid-fifties, Amina has learned to be content with her powerful position as the Emir's first wife, even though she can't claim to have her husband's love anymore. Ever since Karida came into their family, Aliu has gradually loved her, and the things that came from her, more; her children, her advice and her food. She might not have a beautiful body, golden skin and long, curly hair, like Karida, but Amina has authority, as her right.

She put in an effort this morning, to make his breakfast to his liking but still, she can feel the same discontentment emanating from him. On other days, she wouldn't have even bothered about his choosiness; she would have cooked the food to her own liking and not cared what he thought, as long it was pleasing to her, but with the recent chaos whirling around, she has been sympathetic towards him. She is now finished with her breakfast but Aliu has only had a few mouthfuls.

He folds the newspaper towards his left hand, while leaving a finger in between, on the page he was engulfed in. He notices her empty plate and takes one more consolatory taste of the yam and garden-egg sauce before setting his cutlery over it, to signify that he was done. He takes another gulp of cold water and returns his attention to the newspaper.

Since becoming the Emir of Kano, Alhaji Aliu has accepted the fact that every act of religious extremism, within and even beyond his Sultanate, will be, somehow, blamed on him. As it turns out, the attack on the church in Lagos had already been linked to him because of the involvement of a staff under his employ and now, the second attack on a Christian church happened within his state. It is troubling to him, as it no longer seems to be just a rumor that he is influencing these acts of violence. He knows he must make a public statement quickly, as much as he hates talking, to maintain the integrity of his throne.

After swirling the water in his mouth, to properly rinse the food out, Aliu continues reading the Pope's letter printed in the newspaper. In response to the burning of the Saint Thomas Cathedral in Sabon Gari, Kano, Pope Francis had written an open letter, addressed to Nigerians, which was made public this morning:

> '...as I solemnly ask my brothers and sisters, my fathers and mothers, not to be tempted by the wickedness of man and return evil with evil. These conflicts within Nigeria; a country which is just getting ready to rise above all its obstacles; a country which is

commonly referred to as the Giant of Africa; a country blessed with a tremendous deposit of human resources, should be quelled for the divine purpose of peace and progress.

I intreat all those who are in fellowship with the Spirit of our Lord, to emulate his immaculate nature by enduring the present suffering, so that our future of liberty may be secured. For, in time, the truth, the way and the light shall be seen, through the evidence of our actions; through the appearance of our intentions; through the demonstration of our faith.

I implore all Christians, Catholic and Anglican, Pentecostal or Protestant, who may have been involved in the abduction of the Emir of Kano's daughter; Miss Aisha Mustapha, to wash their hands of the Devil's

ways and return the innocent
lady without harm. It is not in
the character of God, his Son,
or the Holy Spirit, to punish
the weak, in order to prove a
point to the strong. We
cannot claim to be fighting
for God; to be fighting the
good fight, when we employ
the mindset of the Devil –'

An introductory knock is heard on the thick
wooden, gold-encrusted door, leading into the main dining
room, from the ground floor hallway. Amina had already
gotten her maid to clear up the dishes and left, while he
was immersed in his reading. The door is opened by the
guard stationed at the entrance and Kabiru, his son, steps
in.

"Good morning, dad," Kabiru greets.

"Good morning," his father responds, turning his
attention back to his paper.

Kabiru has learnt from his mother to always go
straight to the point when in his father's presence. He had
informed Karida about the looming possibility of Hassan's
involvement in Aisha's abduction, after speaking with
Ijeoma, and she had agreed that he go straightaway and
tell the Emir. Kabiru had fallen out of favor with his father
within the last few days but he was hoping he could do

something to regain the lost trust. "It's about Aisha," he starts.

Aliu turns his face back towards him. "What about her?" he asks, perusing his son's countenance, to confirm he wasn't about to receive bad news.

"I just spoke to Pastor John, Aisha's... new boyfriend, and he told me that he suspects Hassan... might be the one who kidnapped Aisha; he said Aisha had just gone to officially end their relationship on Sunday morning. I also spoke to her longtime friend, who knows Hassan too, Ijeoma, and she believes the same thing."

"What do you think?" Aliu asks, nurturing the thought also.

"I think it's very possible. Hassan was very jealous when he heard that Aisha was seeing someone else. He might have done it because she chose John over him."

"...how could I have betrothed my daughter to such an animal?" Aliu asks the air, astounded. "So, you mean that little fool is bold enough to abduct my daughter, at gun point, all because he is jealous?!" he exclaims, not expecting a response. He drops the newspaper, pulls out his chair and stands up, enflamed with vengeance.

"Let me go to Lagos and get to the bottom of this," Kabiru proposes.

"Book a flight and be there today! Find that dog and bring him here to me. If a hair on my daughter's head is missing, he will pay with his life! I don't care what relationship I have with his father," he blares, with confrontation in his eyes, walking towards his son, "as soon as you get to Lagos, a platoon of military-police will be waiting. Take them and search the city thoroughly, until you find him, and force him to reveal where my daughter is! ...all because he has become a mere Major, his wings have outgrown his brain! I will get his Lieutenants to flog him! Thank Allah I didn't join my daughter to a beast!" he spits. He then storms back to his chair to continue with his newspaper. He pulls out the chair and sees Kabiru, still waiting. "Go and get ready now!" he commands.

"Yes, sir," Kabiru replies, inspired by his usually-calm father's expression of authority. He knows this is the chance he has been given to regain the lost trust. He heads out of the dining room determinedly.

*****

Being trapped in an empty, dingy room for almost two days, without even a chair to rest her back on, has almost driven Aisha across the boundary of sanity. She woke up on the dirty floor of the room at night, some hours after she was abducted, greeted with a frightening darkness and bone-piercing cold. She banged the door, twisted the knob frantically and screamed at the top of her lungs repeatedly, for help, but only heard her voice's echo in return. She concluded that she must be in a remote location and all alone, until some hours later, when she heard footsteps; an unknown man unlocked the door of the room and came in, to serve her a plate with two packaged sausage rolls and a sachet of water on it, holding a silver pistol. After the fear that he was going to kill her, had passed, she mustered the courage to ask him 'who are you?' and 'what do you want?' but he didn't answer her questions. He simply warned her not to raise her voice again, dropped her plate on the floor, walked out of the room and locked the door.

Yesterday, she was served two meals by another unknown man, in the late afternoon and at night. She tried to communicate with him also, asking to use a toilet, but he didn't make a sound in response. He dropped her plate of sausage rolls and packaged water on the floor, pointed at the corner of the room and left, holding close to his small machine gun all the time.

Aisha has been in her red dress and red Hijab for almost two days, having to pee at the corner of the small room, on the floor. She has prayed continuously to Allah, to get her out of this hell and return her to her peace; to John, and she is hoping for a favorable answer to her prayers. Yesterday, she had to sleep, for the first time since she gained her consciousness, on the dirty, hard floor, being drained of all her strength and resilience.

Since she woke up, in the early hours of today, she has been in a constant state of panic, wondering what these men will do to her. She is sitting on the floor, hungry, hugging her knees, knowing someone will soon enter to serve her food and hoping today is not the day she dies. The room has only one burglary-proofed window facing the outside of the building and all she can see is a thick bush and large trees, across the distance.

It's late in the afternoon, as the day moves closer to twilight. She hears footsteps again, heading toward her room. She gathers her strength to stand off the floor, before dusting the dirt off her clothes.

The door is unlocked and Abu enters, holding her plate, with two sausage rolls and a sachet of water, and a long machine gun strapped to his shoulder. She looks at him, flabbergasted.

"Abu?" she calls.

"Madam," he replies, bowing his head, humbly and penitently, and holding out her plate.

She approaches him, desperate to confirm if Hassan is the one holding her here; desperate to get a way out. "What have you done, Abu? You betrayed me? So, all this time you've been with me, all the things I've done for you, mean nothing?"

"Madam, please take your food," he pleads, unable to look her in the eyes.

"So, you can sit back and watch them mistreat me? You, who my father hired to guard me? You can treat your Emir's daughter like this?" She gets to him and puts her palm on his shoulder, while his head is still bowed. "Get me out of here, please... get me out and my father will forgive you, and reward you?"

"I am sorry, madam," he lets out, close to tears, "I don't have the power; I have to follow orders." He drops the plate on the floor and kneels. "I didn't want things to be like this."

"Who gave you the orders? Hassan?" she queries, with her hands still on his shoulder, seeing that he still has a conscience.

"Please, madam Aisha, I can't say anything. Just take the food, I beg you."

"So, your loyalty is to these people and not to me? Not to my family? The same people that asked you to attack a church? You face is all over the news; you are a wanted fugitive; the police are after you. Is this the kind of life you want to live? Are these the kind of people you want to be loyal to? They want to destroy your life, so how you can you give them your loyalty? I have shown you nothing but love, Abu! I will never send you out to go and destroy yourself! How can you betray me?!"

"Madam, I'm sorry! I'm sorry, I didn't know it was going to turn like this; I was just following orders…"

"Was it Hassan that ordered you?" she beckons but Abu does not answer. "Tell me! At least tell me that!" she cries.

"That is enough!" comes a voice from outside the room. Aisha looks up and sees a tall man enter. He looks very familiar; she knows she's seen him before. Abu quickly gets off his knees and cleans his teary face with his shoulders.

"I know you," she says to the man, staring at his face and trying to remember him.

"Leave this place, now!" the man commands Abu.

"Yes, sir," Abu replies obediently. He heads out of the room through the open door.

"I saw you," she says to the man, as the memory comes flashing back, "at the Polo Club!"

"Yes, Aisha. I'm Captain Danjuma," he confirms, "the Major will be here soon and he will attend to you."

"Hassan..." she breathes out, livid and terrified at the same time. Danjuma steps out of the room and locks the door.

CHAPTER 14

The dark grey Toyota Corolla speeds down the Ikorodu road, towards Ikorodu town. Rasheed is driving Ijeoma and John towards an unmapped location, where he thinks Hassan might be keeping Aisha. Twilight is slowly giving way for nighttime and John can't help but feel troubled in his spirit; it's like there's a tornado blowing through his chest; his heart is beating fast and he is putting in an effort to breathe steadily.

Ijeoma had called Rasheed, as Kabiru asked her to, but he had travelled to Abuja in the morning for a business meeting, in his father's private jet, and was going to return by five p.m. He also believed that Hassan was capable of abducting Aisha and was eager to help her, so Ijeoma had driven John to the airport, to meet with him as soon as he landed.

Rasheed is hoping, if their suspicions are true, that he would somehow be able save his longtime friend from the heavy hand of justice that is coming for him. He and his friend have done lots of crazy things together, even more when they were younger, but at this point he had dreamed that Hassan would have seen that it was time for them to change and become responsible men, grateful that Allah was merciful enough to overlook their many atrocities and keep them alive. Rasheed has certainly seen the light and he can't compromise his clarity, especially now that he had a wife and a child on the way. He speeds into Ikorodu town, driving Ijeoma's car, heading towards the abandoned warehouse where Hassan and some of his other members were initiated into the Free Assassins secret society. Hassan had taken him there twice; the first time as a friendly gesture, to let his friend know more about himself and the second time during an impromptu operation; a man that his society had been looking for was spotted outside a nightclub on the Lagos Mainland, on a night he followed Hassan out. Hassan called three of his members on phone, who appeared within thirty minutes. They apprehended the man, threw him in the car and drove him to the remote location to finish him off, while Rasheed was in the front passenger seat.

John couldn't help but notice the hostility from Rasheed as soon as they met outside the airport. Rasheed, wearing his expensive silver suit, white shirt button-up shirt and excessive gold accessories, looked at John as though he recognized him but instead of a smile, he sent out a hateful look. John still went ahead to stretch his palm out for a handshake but Rasheed ignored it; he simply greeted Ijeoma with a hug and then started a long conversation with her, before he decided to get into her car and drive them. John has learnt a lot about human behavior, on his way to becoming a Priest, so he sees easily through Rasheed's wall. He knows that he is only mirroring Hassan's hatred for him. Rasheed does not truly hate him;

he has no reason to but he feels it's his duty to make his friend's enemies his own.

Ijeoma's phone rings, cutting through the portentous silence in the car, that has lasted over fifteen minutes. She pulls the phone out of her green leather handbag, beside her legs. It's Kabiru calling.

"Hi, have you landed?" she asks into her phone, leaning back into the front passenger seat, where she hung her purple jacket.

"Yes, I could only get a ticket on the five-pm flight. I'm waiting for the military police to meet up with me here and then we would start our movement. Did you reach Rasheed?"

"Yes. We are in Ikorodu town now; he said he knows where Hassan might be keeping Aisha, so we want to go check it out."

"You and who?" Kabiru asks, suddenly incensed.

"Myself, Rasheed and John."

"Do you know how dangerous that is?" he scolds, "I don't like that idea. Give the phone to Rasheed."

"He's driving – let me put it on speaker." She puts the phone on speaker and holds it up. "Kabiru wants to talk to you," she tells Rasheed.

"Hello," Rasheed says towards the phone in Ijeoma's hand.

"Why would you take Ijeoma with you?" Kabiru protests.

"She met me at the airport – I took her car and left mine behind – aren't you the one that told her to reach me?" Rasheed defends.

"Does that mean you should take her with you? My sister is already missing, you want me to lose her too? Would you take Binta on such a trip?" Kabiru barks.

"It's your sister we're trying to find, so please don't be rude," Ijeoma cuts in, embittered, "and she's my sister too, so I'm not going to sit back and leave it to the boys."

"I told you, I am getting a platoon of military police; why couldn't you just wait for me?"

"We're just going to check the place from a distance, we're not going to go close," Rasheed continues, trying to stop them from arguing, "the place does not have an address, so it's not like I can describe it. Once we get there, we'll have a look and if we see anything suspicious, we'll send you the GPS location, so you can come with the police. It's not like we're going to go in and tell them to release her."

"Once we get there, we'll send you the GPS location," Ijeoma repeats, still bitter, "bye." She cuts the call abruptly. "Nonsense," she hisses, putting the phone down and switching on the radio in her car, "as if he knows better than everyone else."

From the backseat of the car, John watches her tune the radio, frowning, but he is not fooled by her rude countenance; he can tell she really loves Aisha's brother. Some people simply have a different way of feeling and expressing love.

"I'm Josephine Okafor and you're listening to the news at six p.m.," a female voice announces, over the radio. Ijeoma lets go of the tune dial and turns up the volume. "The Emir of Kano's daughter still missing:" Josephine continues, "Miss Aisha Mustapha was abducted by armed men, on Sunday, while leaving her family residence, in Lekki, Lagos. Her black Mercedes Benz was found abandoned on the road, with windows shattered and her driver, Nuru Mohammed, shot dead inside."

All three in the car listen, with ghostly attention, as the matter being discussed publicly couldn't be any more personal to them. They turn off the main road and onto a bushy but tarred road. "I think this is the way..." Rasheed says, making a calculated guess, "but we're still a long way from the warehouse."

"Catholic Church burnt in Kano:" Josephine continues, over the radio, "the Saint Thomas Cathedral in Sabon Gari, Kano, was burnt to the ground last night by a crowd of Muslim religious extremists, who stormed the church with gallons of petrol, claiming that Christians were responsible for the kidnap of their Emir's daughter. The Emir of Kano finally speaks: The Sultan of Kano, Alhaji Aliu Mustapha, sent out a public statement this morning, in the form of a video recording, to Muslims within his Sultanate and to address the nationwide rumors about his involvement in the attack on the Church of Assumption, in Ikoyi, Lagos. Listen to the highlights." A modulated sound can be heard as the Emir speaks; "I do not promote or condone acts of foolishness, like the one that happened yesterday evening in Sabon Gari. Burning down a significant religious establishment under the heel of an assumption, cannot be termed as 'fighting for Allah', it can only be explained as an expression of hatred. My daughter is missing but I haven't blamed any Christian Organization or Union for her abduction – I have reasons to believe that someone close to my family, perpetrated the nefarious act on the Catholic church in Lagos, by having a direct link to my daughter's security guard, Abu Hussein – we are close to uncovering all these issues and as soon as we have incontrovertible evidence, we will present it to the police. Until then, I ask all Muslims to imbibe peace."

*****

The green Mercedes G class parks on the muddy floor, in front of the desolate factory warehouse, beside a black Toyota SUV. Major Hassan turns off his vehicle and steps down, wearing black leather shoes, dark grey jeans and a blue, short sleeve, button-down shirt. He heads straight into the warehouse, as the sun dips under the horizon, eager to finish up what he started. He is quite sure that a few people might be on to him already, as he had received numerous calls from Kabiru today, which he did not pick.

The only weak link he had in the execution of his plans was Abu, who was somehow recognized, but he is sure that as long as Abu remains unfound there will be no evidence of his collusions, only suspicions, and he can live with that.

After another phone conversation with his father, yesterday, he is convinced that the actions of the past week will work together for his good and for the good of the Free Assassins: The rogue military secret society, now headed by his father, with the ultimate aim of controlling the nation. He enters the warehouse, through the creaky metal doors.

"Welcome, Major," Danjuma greets, from the middle of the room.

"Welcome, Major!" Second Lieutenant Rabiu and Lieutenant Danlami salute, as they notice their Major enter.

"At ease," Hassan commands, heading towards them. "Where are Abu and Magaji?" he asks.

"They are on rotation for surveillance, sir" Captain Danjuma, the acting supervisor, explains, "I told them to maintain a five-mile radius around the warehouse and engage or report over radio, if they see anything suspicious."

"That's good. I see you got the factory generator working," he says, appreciating the lit-up warehouse.

"Yes, boss," Danjuma says proudly, "I always get the job done."

"Where is she?" Hassan asks eagerly.

"We kept her in the storage room, sir," Danjuma replies.

"Bring her out. I'll like to talk with her… one last time."

"Yes, sir." Danjuma turns to Danlami and commands; "secure the hostage and bring her out."

"Yes, sir!" Danlami obeys and Rabiu follows him. They head towards the room, at the far end of the enormous warehouse, holding on to their firearms. Rabiu unlocks the door of the storage room, while Danlami pulls out a set of rusty handcuffs from his duty-belt.

It's just over an hour since her last meal, so Aisha is quite sure there must be another reason for the unlocking of the door. She gets up off the dirty floor and dusts herself, feeling unkempt. Rabiu points his automatic rifle at her, while Danlami approaches her holding handcuffs.

"Your hands," Danlami demands of her, holding up the handcuffs in one hand and his silver 44-Magnum pistol in the other hand.

"Hasbi-Allahu wa ni'ma al-wakil," Aisha chants in Arabic, holding out her hands and resigning her fate to Allah. Danlami places the cuffs on her and fastens them.

"Go outside," he gently orders his Major's woman. Aisha complies. She steps out of the squalid room for the first time, slightly relieved but more terrified.

She looks around and notices, for the first time, that she is in an old warehouse, as the roof in her room was not this high. There are pieces of dismantled and rusty machinery all around the large building, which is obviously no longer under maintenance.

She looks across the room and recognizes Hassan, dressed casually, standing beside Danjuma, and all her presumptions are confirmed. She looks him in the face, as she is prodded towards him by the two armed men. He looks back at her, with his usual confident nonchalance. "I knew you were behind this all," she sneers as she approaches him, "and if I could figure it out so easily, I'm sure everyone in my family has too. You'll never get away with this, Hassan."

"Of course, I will," he returns, smiling wryly, "I'm always five steps ahead of you all... you look like you need a bath." He speaks to Danlami; "get another handcuff; cuff both her hands to these two poles here."

"Yes, sir!" Danlami says, before turning to Rabiu to hand over the handcuffs attached to his own duty-belt. He releases the cuffs from one of her wrists and places the second one on it, doing what he was ordered hastily.

"It's only proper that we crucify her, like the so-called Son of God," Hassan continues, mocking, "since she *loves* the Christians so much."

"You weakling, you betrayer!" she spews, close to tears, as the two subordinates stretch her hands apart. "so, you can murder your Emir's daughter... here? After all he has done for your father? Just because I don't love you? I NEVER DID!" Hassan takes three steps forward and slaps her hard on the face.

"How dare you belittle our General?!" he retorts, angered, "what has your coward of a father done for mine? Do you know how many people had to be threatened and assassinated, just so your father could become the Emir? And you little shit, with no home-training, have the boldness to talk down on his name?"

Danlami and Rabiu finish cuffing her hands to the two poles. She stands uncomfortably, with her hands stretched out, as blood runs down the left corner of her lips. "Hasbi-Allahu wa ni'ma al-wakil," she chants, resigning her fate to Allah.

"I don't love you anymore; I don't need your hand in marriage anymore; I certainly don't need a cheating whore as my bride," Hassan proclaims to her, "but at least you will serve a great purpose... after the Christians are blamed for your death, there will be a nationwide riot;

Muslims against Christians… and we, the Free Assassins, will see to it that the conflict grows into all-out chaos. Out of that chaos, a new leader will rise; a strong military leader; General Ibrahim. So, you see, it all works out for our greatness." He stretches his right hand towards Danjuma, while still keeping his eyes on her, and commands; "hand me your pistol."

"Hasbi-Allahu wa ni'ma al-wakil," she chants again, closing her eyes, escaping this hell and finding peace with Allah.

$$*****$$

Rasheed parked less than two kilometers from the abandoned factory, on the untarred, swampy road with thick bushes on both sides. It's some minutes to seven p.m.

He, Ijeoma and John step out. The road ahead goes slightly downhill, so they can see the large building clearly from the distance. The first thing Rasheed noticed before parking was Hassan's green SUV, parked in front of the warehouse, beside another black SUV.

"Well, Hassan is here, so Aisha is most likely here too," Rasheed concludes.

"Maybe I could go around the building and have a look inside," John suggests, considering the geography of the area.

"Do you have a gun on you? Or are you going to perform a miracle like Jesus?" Rasheed asks him mockingly, across the roof of the car.

"No," he replies tersely, not interested in the discourteous banter.

"I didn't think so, so sit back and wait for the police to get here," he sneers. He then turns to Ijeoma. "Have you sent the GPS location to Kabiru?"

"Yes," she responds, reaching in through the passenger door window and dropping her phone into her handbag, "I sent it over text. They're on their way," she says, returning her attention to the building.

John continues to study the landscape from their elevated point, wondering how he can get to the warehouse undetected. He can't bear the thought that Aisha might be in there and in danger, while he is out here, waiting for the police; doing nothing.

"If you move, I spray you now!" comes a hostile voice, from the edge of the thick bush. Rasheed, Ijeoma and John are thunderstruck with panic. A harsh-faced man steps out of the bush, on John and Ijeoma's side, pointing his small automatic rifle. A gun cock is heard from the other side of the road and another man steps out of the thick bush, holding a long AK-47 rifle; it's Abu Hussein. He points his rifle at Rasheed. John, Rasheed and Ijeoma raise their hands in the air. "What you find come here?!" the harsh-faced man demands.

"We were just… going to my friend's house but we got lost," Rasheed replies.

"Lie! I know this one well," Abu reveals to his partner of Rasheed, "and this other one is Pastor John" he says, swinging his rifle towards John.

"You be Pastor John?" the man asks John, to confirm.

"Yes, I am, sir," John replies honestly.

"Great! You might as well tell him why we're here," Rasheed growls, with his hands still in the air, "what is wrong with this idiot?!"

"What else am I expected to say at this point?" John responds, angered by Rasheed's unjustified rudeness.

"Shut up both of you!" Abu commands, "inside the car, now!" The three of them open their doors, ready to enter.

"You, for back!" the man orders Ijeoma. She goes to join John at the backseat, hastily. The man enters the front passenger seat and sits beside Rasheed.

Abu enters the backseat from the driver's side and shuts the door, leaving John sandwiched in between him and Ijeoma.

"Drive!" Abu yells at Rasheed, poking his neck with the long rifle, from the backseat. The other man points his short rifle at John and Ijeoma, from the front, to keep them adequately frightened.

Rasheed starts the car and drives straight on, down the untarred road.

*****

Hassan clutches the black and brown, Ruger Mark IV Lite pistol which he collected from Danjuma, while standing directly in front of Aisha. Blood is trickling from her lips, she is weak, struggling not to rest her weight on her handcuffed wrists and she has her head bowed down;

not wanting to give him the pleasure of seeing her scared. Danlami, Rabiu and Danjuma stand aside watching, unempathetic.

"So, my ex-fiancé, what are your last words?" Hassan enquiries.

Aisha takes her time. She then lets out a frigid, haunting laughter. She raises her head, looks at him and says; "since you asked, I will use my last words wisely, to curse all of you. Your father will *never* rule this country and if he does, his death will be a hundred times more dishonorable than the death you have planned for me. You and every member of your evil cult will be killed like stray dogs!" She looks at the other men. "You're not 'free assassins', there is nothing free about you; you're all just slaves!" She then bows her head again, slowly. "Go ahead and kill me. My heart is with John, even in death."

A car is heard driving into the quiet compound. All four men are given a jolt.

"Rabiu, check," Hassan commands. Rabiu consents speedily. He runs, tiptoeing, towards the main entrance, holding his MP5 rifle in both hands. He peeks out the slightly-open metal door.

"It's Magaji and Abu… look like they catch some people," he relays to his Major. He then opens the door fully, as he sees them all step out of the dark-grey saloon car.

John, Rasheed and Ijeoma are led into the warehouse with their hands raised up, as Magaji and Abu keep their weapons pointed at them.

Hassan waits patiently to see what the cat dragged in, still standing in front of Aisha. She looks towards the door too as the three people are paraded in. The man in front, dressed in all-black, makes her wonder if she's dreaming or if she's dead and doesn't know it yet.

"John?" she whispers, asking the air. Hassan looks at her and then back at the door to confirm if it's really him.

"Boss," Abu announces proudly to Hassan, "we catch this your friend and Pastor John for road."

"Rasheed... you brought them here?" Hassan asks his oldest friend, disappointed, as he notices Ijeoma too.

"Yes, I did, Hassan," he replies, looking him in the eyes lovingly, with his hands still raised up, "because I still believe... that you can change your mind and stop this madness. It's not too late, brother."

"Please, Hassan, just let Aisha go," Ijeoma contributes, lowering her hands carefully and placing her palms together, begging, "please, I know you are angry at her but this is not the solution."

John and Aisha seem to be in a world of their own, communicating with their eyes. She's smiling from her heart, for the first time since she's been here, at him. He's smiling back, happy that his eyes are seeing her alive and believing that, through the divine grace of God that reunited them, they will both escape this place.

Hassan fires his pistol at Ijeoma, sending out a shockingly loud, echoing sound through the hollow warehouse, and the bullet pierces her left shoulder, just above her heart. She screams and falls to the ground. Aisha screams too. "You brought her here!" he yells at Rasheed, "I trusted you with my secrets and you told it to my enemies?! So, you're now on their side?! You're on his side?!" he questions Rasheed, swinging his pistol and pointing it at John's head.

Rasheed ignores him, drops down crouching and attends to Ijeoma who's on the floor, bleeding profusely and in pain. Her white top is gradually being stained, as her blood permeates it. He raises her head off the hard ground and places it on his thighs before taking off his white corporate shirt and placing it on her wound. He then puts her palm over it, with his, and helps her apply pressure, while she gasps and sobs, in pain. "ARE YOU CRAZY?!" he screams at Hassan, with tears running down his face, "THIS IS KABIRU'S WOMAN! She is one of us!"

"I don't care about Kabiru anymore," he drops emotionlessly, marching towards John, "or his girlfriend, or any member of his family." He grabs John by the collar, ignoring Rasheed, jabs the butt of his pistol into the temple of his skull and drags him towards Aisha. "So, this is the fool you chose over me?!" he asks her.

"Yes, I chose him... and I don't regret it," she responds defiantly, only considering John's face and not his.

"This little boy?" he jibes, enraged.

"He's more of a man than you'll ever be; you're the boy," she asserts.

"Let's see about that." He shoves John towards one of the metal pillars before stretching the pistol towards Danjuma and commanding; "Hold!" Captain Danjuma steps forward, collects his pistol from the Major and then steps back.

"I'll give you a chance to save your lover," he says to John, who's still recovering from his ribs being jarred against the hard pillar, "beat me and I'll let both of you go," he continues, clenching his fists, "I'll even let you take your two new friends here," he says, pointing at Rasheed and Ijeoma on the floor.

Father John knows he can't best Hassan in a fist fight but he clenches his fists too, preparing himself for a pounding, knowing that the Lord is in control and ultimately, he is hoping that he would be able to delay Hassan long enough for the police to get here. He approaches Hassan.

Hassan launches a heavy righthand punch, connecting with his left cheek. John's neck is sent twisting and his body follows, while blood spurts out of his mouth. He quickly tries to regain composure, knowing Hassan won't give him time to recover, even though the world is whirling before his eyes.

Hassan dashes towards him and teases him with a left jab before throwing another heavy right punch. John follows his natural instincts and defends himself; stepping backwards, crouching and defending his face with the back of his hands, from the elbows to the fists. Hassan doesn't relent; he continues swinging punches, from the left and from the right, while John tries his best to defend.

While still crouching, John charges into him and springs himself upwards, throwing a heavy righthand uppercut which connects sweetly with the bottom of his jaw. Hassan is sent backwards, giving John a little time to recover.

"Nice," Hassan lauds, gaining his balance, before spitting out blood, "at least you can throw a punch." He then gets back to his fighting stance and approaches John steadily.

John blocks his face again and steps backwards, expecting Hassan to come at him with heavy punches but instead Hassan thrusts a heavy kick at him. His back is shoved against a piece of rusty machinery and before he can recover from the pain, Hassan grabs his throat with his left hand and rams his skull into the machine; John almost goes unconscious. Hassan keeps his left hand on his throat, while he is still dizzy, and begins to pound his face with his right fist, again and again.

He then stops and lets go of John's neck, allowing him fall to the ground with his face bloodied.

John tries to crawl away while coughing and gasping for air, with his back, face and skull aching, but Hassan kicks his hands, causing him to fall on his face. He then steps on his skull.

"Who is the man now?!" he shouts at Aisha, who has been twisting around in her cuffs to watch the fight, terrified for John.

"You'll always be a boy, Hassan," she replies, with tears in her eyes for John, "because you are not mature enough to understand love. Even if you kill a thousand men, you're still a boy."

"Enough of this nonsense!" he exclaims, leaving John on the floor and marching towards Danjuma to collect the pistol, "I'll finish what I started." He snatches the Mark IV pistol from Danjuma and points it at Aisha's head, approaching her.

"Noo!!" John pleads, struggling off the floor. Aisha closes her eyes.

"Boss, no!" Abu protests, while cocking his rifle and pointing it at Hassan. Danjuma, Magaji, Rabiu and Danlami look at him incredulously. Hassan also turns his face toward him, hearing the gun cock.

"Are you pointing your rifle at me?" he asks, insulted, with his pistol still pointed at Aisha.

"Boss – Major, please, leave Madam," Abu retorts, shakily.

"Lower your firearm, now!" Captain Danjuma commands Abu.

"Boss, please, I swear to the Emir, say I will protect his daughter. It's because of me she is here. Please, just keep her inside cell or carry her anywhere but don't kill her."

"And what of the oath you swore here, to the Free Assassins?" Danjuma queries his subordinate.

"Swear not suppose cancel swear. I not fit let you kill her," Abu concludes.

"Is it because we allowed this cadet to join us that he has the courage to raise his firearm at me?!" Hassan growls.

"Abu, drop your gun now!" Lieutenant Danlami commands, pointing his Magnum-Revolver pistol at Abu.

"Drop it!" Rabiu adds, standing beside Danlami, pointing his MP5 rifle at Abu too.

"Abu, why you doing this?" pleads Magaji, who is standing beside him.

Abu fires two bullets from his AK-47 rifle. Rabiu and Danlami, who are to the left of Hassan, drop dead as the bullets enter their skulls. He then quickly returns his aim to the Major, who still has his pistol pointed at Aisha.

Magaji raises his own MP5 rifle quietly and blows Abu's head open from close range. He falls to the ground, lifeless, as his blood and particles of his brain are sprayed on Rasheed and Ijeoma close by.

The sound of sirens can be heard in the distance as the warehouse quiets down. Hassan lowers his pistol and looks towards his Captain, before looking at Rasheed.

Rasheed has been tending to Ijeoma, whose life is slowly slipping away. He wasn't even concerned with the blood splashed on him. "If I was you, I would start running. Kabiru is coming here with over forty military-policemen," Rasheed says, after glancing at Hassan and then turning his attention back to Ijeoma on his thighs.

"Go and check," Hassan requests of Magaji.

"Yes, sir." It's dark already as Magaji peeks out the entrance. He can see the multiple siren lights whirling in the darkness, from the top of the hill. He turns back inside. "They're coming here," he informs Hassan and Danjuma.

"So, you led Kabiru here too?!" Hassan yells at Rasheed, irate.

"The Emir knows, the police know," Rasheed says calmly, "I came here first, thinking I could appeal to your last shred of humanity... but you've obviously lost that too.

The best thing you can do now is gather your remaining men and run."

"I have over a hundred thousand Free Assassins to protect me!"

"Well, unless they're here right now, running is still your best option."

"Boss, they're getting close," Magaji humbly informs.

"Evacuate," Hassan commands. Danjuma and Magaji head outside the warehouse while Hassan remains.

"She's dying," Rasheed says of Ijeoma, with tears.

Hassan ignores him and walks over to Aisha. He puts his pistol to her head. "You're the reason for all this," he whispers to her. She looks back at him defiantly.

"Please, please!" John intercedes.

"Hassan! Run, now," Rasheed advises.

"Major, we need to go!" Captain Dajuma pleads, standing at the entrance, "our objective has been foiled. We were supposed to blame her death on the Christians..."

"HAAAH!" Hassan roars. He then runs out of the warehouse to join his partners.

The sirens are much closer now. Hassan starts his SUV and screeches away. Captain Danjuma also starts the black SUV and follows. They drive out of the compound hastily.

John, who is still in pains, finally gets a chance to embrace Aisha. He then looks on the floor and pulls a handcuff key off the belt of one the deceased men close by. He uncuffs both her hands. She is well drained of energy too, so she falls into his arms.

"I love you," she says.

"I love you," he says too.

"Ijeoma," Aisha then calls, worried. She and John support each other as they hobble toward her and Rasheed.

Some of the police vehicles can be seen pulling into the compound, through the open main entrance. Some military-policemen step down, pointing their rifles, wearing thick body armor and helmets. They enter the lit-up ware house, observing the dead bodies. "Hands up!" they announce.

No one seems to have the energy or desire to obey. Aisha and John just get to Rasheed and Ijeoma.

"They just left," John manages to explain, "these ones killed themselves."

Kabiru comes rushing in and sees everyone. "IJEOMA!" he screams. "What happened to her?" he asks everyone, as he kneels beside her.

"Hassan shot her," Aisha replies.

"You bastard!" he yells at Rasheed "I told you not to take her!"

"I'm sorry, man," Rasheed pleads, crying profusely, "things got out of hand." Kabiru carefully puts her on his own thigh before shoving Rasheed away violently. Rasheed's silver pants are soaked with her blood and he is only wearing his singlet on top. The white button-up shirt he used to cover her wound is now completely soaked red, so is her white top.

"Baby," Kabiru says to her, frantic, "I'll get you to a hospital now."

"Don't worry, love... it's okay... everything is... okay now."

"I told you not to go. Why don't you listen to me?" he scolds, with his eyes watery.

"That's why you love me... isn't it?" she replies, smiling at him through her pain.

"Let's get to the hospital."

"No, no... I only have a few moments left. Just... just listen."

"Don't say that, please," he beseeches. Aisha, John and Rasheed standby, watching and listening.

"You're the first person I ever loved... you're the... only person I've ever loved... and... I'll always... love you."

*****

The end-of-the-year faculty barbecue nights were always a must-go for every student in the University of Lagos. All the departments in each of the nine faculties came together to organize their own nighttime party, which attracted all the students within their faculty and beyond. Each barbecue night would be highlighted by loud music, live performances, barbecued meat, fish, chicken and turkey, as well as various cocktails; mostly alcoholic.

The goal of every young vibrant male was to get tipsy – or drunk – and dance with as many girls as possible, preferably the girls they were crushing on. John had always been a little different from the crowd; he only came to the barbecue parties to observe and mingle from a distance. He did go to almost every one of them because he happened to live on campus and his uncle and guardian; Prof. Amaechi, encouraged him to experience life.

From his own distant corner, holding an alcoholic cup of cocktail, he would have a dashingly exciting time. His eyes and ears were always enough to sense and experience a superior amount of the event; he hardly ever got to dance with any girl and he usually came alone, from home.

This night, his faculty; the Faculty of Arts, was throwing their own barbecue night, at their large faculty parking lot, and John had no reason not to attend. He ordered his second cup of alcoholic cocktail, after queueing for up to fifteen minutes, and retreated to the edge of the dancing crowd, from where he continued to observe anonymously.

There were about two thousand young people buzzing around each other; most dancing, some queuing up to buy barbecue and cocktails, some engulfed in seemingly exciting conversation, some in motion; navigating their way through the sea of dancing people and others hanging around at the edges like himself.

John had been there for over an hour, vicariously enjoying what everyone around him was enjoying, when he looked towards his right and saw the last person he was expecting to see at the Faculty of Arts barbecue night, or any other barbecue night. She was standing about twenty meters away, at the edge of the crowd too, with her face obscured by her white Hijab but he could spot her from her usually calm posture and her taller, light skinned friend; Ijeoma, who was standing beside her.

'What is Aisha doing in school?' he thought to himself before realizing that he was already walking towards her. He had known her for up to two months and he could claim that they had become good friends. He knew she never stayed in school past six or seven p.m., he knew she had never spent a night in the female hostels before and he knew she had no plans of coming to his faculty's barbecue night because they hung out today and she didn't mention it.

Out of all the people he could think of that night, she was the only person he didn't mind socializing with. Every time they hung out, he didn't feel weird or geeky about expressing his deeply kept opinions of life and the universe; ideas he spent a lot of quiet time philosophizing about, and most of all, he loved her opinions of things too.

"Did you miss your way home this evening?" he jibed, as he got to her.

Aisha turned towards the familiar voice sharply and then laughed. "Just the person I was hoping to see! – I guess you can say that."

"Hi," he offered Ijeoma, who had a happy face on too.

"John," she replied, waving at him across Aisha.

"I was just thinking of calling you, to find out if you were here," Aisha said.

"I can't miss my own faculty barbecue night," he defended, "I usually go to all the barbecue nights, it's just a stroll away from home and it beats watching TV or playing video games – how come you're here?" he asked, curious.

"It's my brother o! All because my mother travelled to Abuja this morning, he decided to steal one of the cars and come to school for the Faculty of Arts Barbecue night, so I threatened that I'll report him unless he takes me along." She giggled mischievously. He chuckled happily. "Yeah, it's all Kabiru's fault I'm here."

"Well, thank your brother for being naughty tonight. It's nice to have you here," he let out.

"It's nice to be in school at this time. I never knew Unilag students could be this wild!" she exclaimed, taking in the view of the dancing crowd.

"Yes, with a little darkness and some alcohol, they can be this wild," he enlightened, turning towards the crowd too and taking a sip from his cup.

"What are you drinking?"

"Cocktail – it's alcoholic."

"Let me try it," she said, reaching for his cup. He handed it to her. "I've never tried alcohol before... but then I've never been in school this late either." She took a swig of the drink. He watched her analyze the taste in her mouth. She then shrugged. "Not bad," she gave, returning the plastic cup to him.

"Hold on to that, let me get more," he offered, rejecting the cup. He then turned to Ijeoma. "Do you want one?" he asked.

"Yes please," she replied.

"Okay," John dropped. He turned to leave, while smiling briefly at Aisha. She smiled too, with a spark of happiness in her eyes.

She watched him leave hurriedly, while taking another swig of the sweet cocktail with a bitter aftertaste. She then turned her attention to the energetic crowd.

"So, you dragged me out of my hostel at night, just so I could escort you to meet John," Ijeoma grunted.

"What?!" Aisha breathed out, smiling defensively.

"I'm not angry, I just don't like being a third wheel."

"I called you because we are best friends and this is my first night in school, so I needed your guidance – are you planning to ditch me?"

"Here you go, sweetie. I got you chicken," Kabiru endeared Aisha, holding out a disposable pack. She and Ijeoma turned towards him.

"What's this for?" she asked, collecting the pack and looking at him suspiciously.

"For keeping your mouth shut," he replied bluntly, "and... for dancing with your friend." He threw a smile at Ijeoma. "Do you want to dance?" he asked her, holding out his palm.

She smiled back. "Yeah," she said, putting her palm in his. She swung her head over her shoulder at Aisha, as Kabiru led her into the dancing crowd. "You'll have more fun without me," she threw, with a guilty smile.

She immediately forgave Ijeoma for not wanting to babysit her tonight. She knew she was in reliable hands with John. She downed the rest of the cocktail in the plastic cup and dropped it. She then opened the disposable pack to confirm its contents; chopped, barbecued chicken.

"Where is Ijeoma?" John asked, as he returned, holding two full cups in his right hand and another in his left hand.

"She is on the dancefloor with my brother," she replied, relieving his right hand of one cup.

"Oh, he knows her?" he asked, looking at Ijeoma and Kabiru dancing a slight distance away, before taking a sip from the cup in his left hand.

"No, they just met this evening, when we went to pick her up but I guess... she was just bored," Aisha defended, taking a sip of cocktail from her fresh cup. They both turned their attention back to the crowd, standing side by side.

"You've finished the other cup?" he asked, stunned.

"Yeah."

"Number one rule of drinking alcohol; don't rush it," he cautioned, "most especially, if you're drinking for the first time. I suggest you spend an hour on this new cup."

"An hour?" she asked, befuddled.

"Yes. This isn't a soft drink, it's alcoholic. I'm sure I don't need to tell you one of the many stories about how people got drunk and misbehaved."

"Okay. You know better, so an hour it is," she conceded, before taking a gentle sip from her cup. They continued, taking in the view of young vibrant people; most of them seeking some form of temporary escape.

"Soooo," he drew, looking towards her, holding a cup in each hand. She looked back at him expectantly. "Do you want to dance? I wouldn't mind if you said no but I'll still feel bad if you said no."

"No… sorry," she consoled, "I don't do the whole 'dancing in public' thing."

"Oh, well… it's okay," he managed, trying to be understanding, "I'm a horrible dancer, so I was hoping you wouldn't give me a chance to embarrass myself – but what's so bad about dancing?"

"It's not bad, I just don't feel comfortable shaking my bum-bum in public," she elucidated, "I mean; a woman's body is a source of temptation to men; a source of distraction. We've all known that since Adam and Eve, so a woman is supposed to assist the men by behaving modestly; cover herself properly and carry herself gracefully. I mean, if you look at it, it also boils down to getting respect from the opposite sex; if all men see you as is 'sexy', then that's all they're going to think about you; sex, and every time you stand up for respect or power, they'll just laugh – I mean; I can't even stand the idea of a guy staring at my body parts when I'm walking down the road, talk more shaking it all over this public place – no!"

"Well, your friend is shaking it on the dancefloor, why didn't you tell this to her?"

"Like I said, dancing is not bad, I just don't feel comfortable. We were talking about me and not Ijeoma – maybe you have a crush on her," she spilled.

"Her?! No way!"

"Did I just say that? – I think I'm getting... drunk. Is this what alcohol does to people?"

"Yeah, it's an ancient truth serum," he jibed.

"I... obviously know you don't have a crush on Ijeoma, so maybe not a truth serum... but a serum of some kind," she slurred, looking into her cup

'I have a crush on you,' John thought about saying.

"I have to pee – and I just said that out loud... anyway, can you escort me and be my bodyguard? I've heard scary stories about Unilag at night."

"Unilag isn't that bad," he advocated, leading the way. She instinctively followed. "I live on campus and I've hardly ever heard reports about guys... molesting girls, but maybe, about ten years ago –"

"Where are we going?"

"Inside the Arts faculty," he explained, stepping onto the sidewalk that led towards the faculty entrance, "the student's toilets are closed by now but I know there's a clean lecturer's toilet open on the top floor."

"Clean is the selling point here," she said, walking closely behind him, "clean is the reason why I'm going to take another risk of getting expelled, with you!"

"Which other time did you do that?"

"When you helped me *cheat* in my exam!"

"That was for a good cause, just as this is," he clowned, stepping through the main entrance to the Arts faculty. He headed for the central staircase.

"What's good about this cause?"

"The modest lady needs a clean toilet – sympathetic enough – I've been drinking too, don't mind me," he announced, dropping one of the cups after finishing the contents. He then took a sip from the fresh cup in his right hand.

"Who am I to judge?" She took a sip from her cup too, as they climbed onto the first floor.

"So... you were talking about Adam and Eve and the whole woman being a temptation to man," he started.

"Yeah," she urged.

"I think that it's the duty of the man to overlook the temptation of the woman's body. It takes strength and that's what becoming mature is about. Women can't always babysit us by covering their bodies, we are going to see and we should be able to see without being distracted. Like, in the garden of Eden, before man fell, they were both naked but didn't realize it. I think men have to become mature to rediscover that kind of innocence and then they can have meaningful communication with women."

"Hmmm," she let out, analyzing his idea, "I'm hoping for the day we 'return to Eden' but for now we are in the University of Lagos, in Nigeria, and the last time I checked men were still babies." They got to the top floor. The toilet John was referring to was just a few steps away.

He looked across the left and right side of the balcony corridor before saying; "You see, the coast is clear. There you go – I'll guard the area, madam."

"Good boy. Help me hold these," she returned, handing him her cup and disposable pack.

"I'll like to think I'm a mature man," he pressed jovially.

"Good man, then." She headed into the toilet and shut the door.

He walked towards the edge of the balcony, close by, with two cups in his right hand and the disposable pack in his left. The faculty of Arts block was made of two identical four-story buildings facing each other, with balcony corridors on each floor, and connected by three staircases; one at the center and two at the edges. John had spent almost three years as a student in this school and was in the final semester of his three hundred level, but he hadn't gotten his fill of the social experience. He disdained the idea of losing himself to the crowd but he knew he was in need of an indelible mark; an indelible memory; a cosmic shift that would reshape his life and give him lasting form. These few moments with Aisha made him feel like he was on his way to having it all.

"The music is so loud from up here," she said, shutting the toilet door. He turned to face her.

"Yes, it is. Was it clean?" he asked.

"Uh-hmmm," she confirmed, "they even had hand wash. Wish all students toilets were that clean."

He handed her the disposable pack and her cup. "And we didn't get caught," he bragged. She smiled. He led the way, down the stairs.

She followed, taking a sip of her cocktail. "You're the one spoiling me; teaching me how to break the rules."

"I'm not, honestly," he protested, "I'm not trying to spoil you; I like the fact that you're a good girl and I want you to remain one, I'm just... showing you... a few more possibilities."

"Good girl," she thought aloud, "I would like to be a bad girl too... sometimes – not in public though. I mean; I guess I'll be able to be a bad girl with my husband." She was about to take another sip when she spurted; "I hope I'll be able to be a bad girl with my husband."

*****

"It's been eight days since Aisha Mustapha has been found; the Emir of Kano's daughter," Nkechi Ejiofor says, opening the discussion for her two co-hosts, "we have learnt that Major Hassan Ibrahim, a person she had been betrothed to, was responsible for her abduction and also for the failed attack on Father John, within the Church of Assumption rectory. Major Hassan was intercepted by the military police, while trying to flee their hideout in Ikorodu, where they had kept Miss Aisha. A fierce gun exchange ensued as they maneuvered their way through the busy parts of Ikorodu town; fourteen bystanders got hit by stray bullets. Major Hassan was later killed along with a member of his gang; Second Lieutenant Magaji. Captain Danjuma, who was also fleeing with them, was captured and has been in police custody ever since... there have also been various allegations against General Musa Ibrahim, as being the leader of his son's gang; a secret society within the Nigerian Army, but the Nigerian police are yet to determine if this is true."

"I hear the DSS has stepped in," Kunle adds, "to take over the investigation. The Presidency has obviously been rocked by the news that there is a rogue society within the Army, planning a coup. I don't believe anyone here wants to return to the eighties, nineties when we were under military rule. Those were dark ages and I commend the government for taking this seriously. If these people are out there, we need to uncover them and uproot them quickly."

"As we can see, we were all being played," Kemi contributes, "by ruthless men, who simply wanted to spread hate amongst us and drive us to the point of blindness, so that they could rob us easily. Power-hungry animals, with no care for human life. Certainly, we are better off not being ruled by such people; people who have no care for our welfare. People like Major Hassan, and possibly his father, who have the freedom to take the law into their own hands; launch an attack on a religious organization and abduct the Emir's daughter; his supposed fiancé."

"Miss Aisha Mustapha had never made a public affair of her relationship with Major Hassan. Only members of her family knew that they were betrothed; they hadn't been any ceremony to mark their engagement, not even social media posts of them together. She might have been putting him off, only for him to discover that she was in love with someone else."

"If we were still wondering what was going on between Miss Aisha and Father John, she made it quite clear to us with her Instagram post, yesterday evening," Nkechi announces excitedly, "she posted a picture of herself cuddled up with Father John, some hours after he was discharged from the Reddington Hospital, in Victoria Island. Underneath the picture, she wrote this charming message:

> 'Seven days ago, I lost my longtime and closest friend. I can't help but feel that she gave her life for me. Ijeoma, I pray to Allah that you rest in peace. Seven days after you are gone and seven days after I was released from the hands of that monster, I write to all Nigerians; this message of resurrection, love and peace. Resurrection because Ijeoma will not

remain dead; she will be reborn in my heart, in the hearts of everyone that loved her and in the hearts of everyone reading this. Love because John and I have been in love for years, even though we've been apart most of the time. We are not asking for much; we just want to be together. Love can never be an evil thing. Love came before religion; before man fell, sinned and was given the law to abide by; in the garden of Eden, when man first saw woman, he loved her and she loved him back. Peace because our union will only make us stronger; truth joined with truth will only result in more truth. John is my peace, just as I am his, and I hope our union will be a sign of peace to everyone in the world.'

There is a knock on the door. Alhaji Aliu Mustapha, looks toward his bedroom entrance and away from the television, unable to contain his smile of pride. It's a beautiful morning and he decided to have his breakfast in bed. He is expecting a well-cooked meal, as usual, from his favorite wife.

"Come in," he confirms.

Karida opens the door slightly and pops her head in, smiling.

THE END.

Take a Picture with your copy of Aisha and John and tag
@OlufemiTheGreat on Instagram

Fan Mail: olubalogun11@gmail.com

Printed in Great Britain
by Amazon

34645027R00192